JAMAAL THE IT GUY

JAMAAL THE IT GUY

Kasha Thompson

WEBSTER AVENUE PUBLISHING
SACRAMENTO, CA

JAMAAL THE IT GUY

Paperback ISBN: 979-8-9862679-5-1

Copyright 2024 Kasha Thompson

This book is a work of fiction. Names, characters, places, and incidents are the product of the author's imagination or are used fictitiously. Any resemblance to actual events, locales, or persons, living or dead, is strictly coincidental.

This edition published and arranged by Webster Avenue Publishing.

Printed in the United States of America. First Edition June 2024.

Character Illustration: Volhah via iStock

Cover Design by: Webster Avenue Publishing

Interior Layout by: Webster Avenue Publishing

Editing: Courtney Driver of Whoproofedit.com

black love nov·el·ette

/blak/ /ləv/ /nävəˈlet/

noun

1. a short novel, typically one that is light and romantic or sentimental in character.

2. an amuse-bouche story centered around Black love with just the right amount of sweet, savory, and spice.

Content Notes

Please note Jamaal the IT Guy discusses topics which could potentially trigger certain audiences. Some readers may consider the following as spoilers.

Moderate coarse language
Several sexually explicit scenes

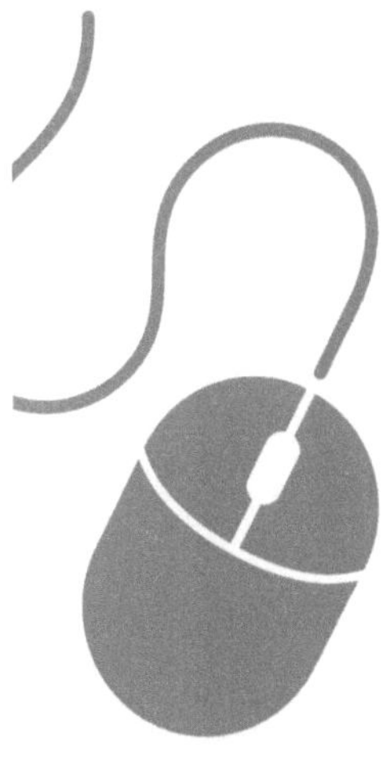

1

I WAS RUSHING THROUGH THE CAMPUS OF CODEABILITY with two black coffees, three iced lattes, one matcha tea, a chocolate chip scone, and a cup of oat milk. The main building had coffee but Jerrika Reese, my supervisor, wanted the good stuff from the Bean There Done That in the Invictus building, which was halfway across the property. With hurried steps, I maneuvered my way back over the busy square while trying my best not to spill a drop.

When I got the job offer to be the assistant to Miles Graves, the owner of Codeability, I was on cloud nine. But it turned out I was more of the assistant to Miles's personal assistant. So my contact with Mr. Graves was limited and with three months on the job, I doubted he knew my name, even though I greeted him each morning with a bright smile and his favorite energy drink.

In spite of all that, Codeability was one of the hottest tech firms in San Diego. It sat on close to fifty acres with two large buildings and several smaller structures that housed the various divisions along with meeting rooms, conference centers, and restaurants. The campus was designed to encourage employees to stay on the grounds because everything you needed was provided on-site. Just hop on one of the many free bicycles or electric scooters parked throughout the campus and you could hit up the gym, game room, or one of the sleeping pods.

Back at the main building staffers called the Brain Trust, because it housed some of the biggest minds in the tech game, I made my way to the top floor. Jerrika and the others were in one of the glass conference rooms going over next month's event calendar.

"Good afternoon, who's ready for a midday pick me up?" I circled the room, passing out drinks. Crème brûlée latte for Joel, black coffee for Tara. I handed the final drink to my boss, who opened her always glossed mouth. "You're welcome," I said, in anticipation of a thank you that never came.

Jerrika cast her eyes toward me. "What?"

"Umm, you're welcome to let me know if you need anything else." I smiled to hide the mortification forming on my face. With my size seven foot firmly imbedded in my mouth, which was commonplace for me, I gathered the trash and quickly returned to my desk. When I first started, I thought Jerrika didn't like me, but I soon learned she barely liked anyone. If you couldn't do something for her, she wasn't going to waste her time.

The last few months consisted of Jerrika barking orders and me taking it. To her, everything was a rush, mostly because she lacked time management. Her failure to properly plan often ended with me having to fix her self-inflicted errors. Several weeks ago, Jerrika was responsible for hiring a DJ for one of our social events. Days before, she came to me insisting I dropped the ball on a task I was never assigned.

Do you know how difficult it is to book a DJ during the summer in California? I was able to avert the crisis by begging my roommate to DJ the gig. Was Simone a DJ? No. But she did have an eclectic taste in music and a plucky can-do attitude. *Did she play any songs from the last twenty years?* No. But her eighties playlist was still a hit.

Back at my desk on top of my pile of papers was Jerrika's laptop with a note.

THIS COMPUTER IS A PIECE OF CRAP.

HAVE *IT* FIX IT OR GET ME A NEW ONE ASAP.
J.R

Pinching the brim of my nose, I exhaled a pained breath. Jerrika's vocabulary lacked the words please and thank you. Shit I would have accepted a crudely drawn smiley face. Since I'd been hired, I was more of her gofer than anything else. Don't get me wrong, I get it. I was the assistant to the assistant, but I assumed my day would consist of helping to write reports and respond to event invites. Nowhere in the job description did it list purchasing pregnancy tests and picking up Jerrika's dry cleaning.

When I was hired at Codeability it was all about getting my foot in the door. I was willing to start at the bottom because I knew I was more than capable of climbing to the top. Having graduated magna cum laude from UC Davis with a degree in communications and marketing, assistant to the assistant was a stepping stone for me. Eventually I'd be the one with an assistant. And I can assure you I would never make them walk clear across campus no matter how yummy the coffee was.

This latest menial assignment was one I was actually looking forward to. In my brief time with the company, I'd learned the foosball table wasn't level, so if you played on the left side you'd have an advantage. If you wanted to be alone, Allen Hall was the place to do it. When there wasn't a big event it was often a ghost town. And lastly, Jamaal from IT could crack my spine like a book any day of the week.

Sifting through my purse, I added a hint of pink gloss to my lips. The aim was to look like I'd just eaten a popsicle and the juices from the artificial strawberry flavoring tinted my pucker. I swept the eye boogers from the corners of my lids and popped a mint before grabbing the laptop and making a trip down to the basement. The basement was composed entirely of the Information Technology division. A technology company like this one needed a strong tech team and the men and women on the underground floor were like the ninety-seven Dream Team ... of geeks.

In the elevator, I fussed with my braids, wanting them to fall just right. Looking down at my blouse, I made sure the girls were sitting at attention. Normally I didn't care much about my appearance, but on my first day of work I sat through a forty-five-minute IT security and awareness presentation hosted by the finest man I'd ever laid eyes on. And since that day I was plotting ways to see him again, and Jerrika had just given me the perfect excuse.

When the elevator doors opened, I made a left and entered the IT sanctuary. This place was a maze of glass walls. In the distance, the sound of clicking keyboard keys and faint laughter met my ears. Ambling up to the helpdesk, I waited in line behind a blonde woman who looked like she was still in high school. Craning my neck beyond the line, I scanned the area hoping to spot Mr. Geek Squad. He wouldn't be hard to identify, his umber skin standing out in a sea of lighter faces.

The queue moved quickly. Most people submitted their IT concerns virtually, but if I did that I would miss the chance to ogle the help.

At the front of the line, I was greeted by an unamused gentleman. "How can I help you?"

"My supervisor is having issues with her laptop." I lifted the small metal rectangle, giving it a shake.

"What seems to be the problem?"

"That's a good question." Only now was I realizing I had no clue what the issue was. Jerrika's note provided a directive with zero details. I probably should have asked some follow-up questions before rushing down here all dehydrated.

"You don't know what the problem is?" His eyes narrowed.

"Not exactly. It could be a restart issue or I know she was having trouble with her bookmarks. It could be that." My face brightened seeing an opportunity. "You know last time there was a problem Jamaal helped me. Is he available?" I focused my attention behind the intake clerk at the desk. Standing on my tiptoes, I searched the space once more.

"Name?"

"Winifred Chambers."

"Have a seat and someone will be with you shortly."

"Preferably Jamaal." I smiled sweetly.

The clerk nodded toward the waiting area before moving to the next person in line.

Taking a seat, I waited, tempted to search for a reflective surface to confirm my melanin rich skin was still popping. Since starting with the company, I'd enlisted the help of the IT department frequently. Shortly after becoming aware of Jamaal's existence, my need for technical support rose exponentially. Login issues, sticky keys, lost bookmarks, a malfunctioning camera, sand in the keyboard. I'm not proud to admit it, but some of the technical issues were woman made.

All for a good reason, to see the fine ass bespeckled computer nerd. He was tall. Well taller than me, which wasn't hard to accomplish even when I was rocking heels. And when he assisted me he was always so pleasant. He spoke slowly like each word that passed through his lips was sacred as he explained every step. And while I didn't understand half of the technical jargon he was using, I could sit and listen to this man talk for hours. I imagined his easy speech pattern would be perfect for talking me through the mind-numbing orgasms only he could administer.

It also afforded me the chance to etch each one of his features to memory. His long, meticulously neat fingers would point out all the sand hidden under the keys of my keyboard. The way he'd licked the left corner of his perfect mouth after a sip of coffee. Just the left side, never the right. If I was lucky, some days his button up was replaced by a polo shirt and I could watch his strong arms flex and stretch and I imagined them wrapped around me. And just like that, my focus would drift to what it would feel like if he fucked me on top of his office desk and not on how he debugged my main frame.

"Mrs. Chambers?" a familiar voice called.

I jumped up from my seat. "Here, that's me."

"Did I get that correct? Is it … Mrs.?"

He'd never asked for clarification before. "It's Miss actually. But it's fine."

A smile played at the corners of his lips. "No, I apologize. Miss Chambers, how can I help you?"

"I have problems."

His eyelids fell to half-mast.

"Not me, the computer is giving me problems. Actually it's not even my laptop, it's my supervisor's computer and she has problems."

"Okay, I can help with that. Just follow me." He turned, walking past the help desk into the hub of IT.

I would follow his peach-shaped ass anywhere. Which was an insane statement to make when all I knew about him was he was super smart, smelled like spicy ginger with a hint of orange blossoms, and had immaculately clean hands. Hands that on more than one occasion I'd envisioned roaming my body.

His stride was slow and deliberate, ensuring I didn't get outpaced by his long legs. Normally he would lead me to one of the nondescript service cubes, but they must have all been occupied because we turned right instead of remaining straight and ended up at his desk. He motioned to a seat. His cube was just how I imagined it, meticulous. Not a wayward pen or paper clip. Everything had a place. Jamaal's desk was a stark contrast to mine, which was way too kitschy. I'd amassed quite the collection of Codeability merchandise in my short three months here. I'm talking mugs, stress balls, notepads, and tumblers. I even had a highly coveted Miles Graves bobble head.

"Can I?" He held out his hand.

For a split second I was tempted to offer him my hand in

return. But it was clear he was interested in the laptop and not planting kisses up my arm like the cartoon skunk that liked to sexually harass cats.

Turning over the laptop, I waited patiently as he rebooted the system. While he did, I examined his workspace for signs of a girlfriend, like a cute picture or a card with hearts. I spotted a photo, but it wasn't what I was expecting. On his desk was a framed photograph of a cat. It was one of those wrinkled cats with no hair and the expression on its face was something out of a horror movie.

"Is that your cat?" I asked, pointing at the framed feline on his desk.

"No, umm it's a long story."

My eyebrows inched upward, hoping he'd share. The longer the better. If we needed, we could always continue the discussion during dinner and finish it over breakfast.

"I lost a bet and as a result I have to look at this hideous cat for the next six months." He scratched at his elbow. "I guess that wasn't really a long story at all. In the future I should just explain instead of making it out to be some epic tale."

"What was the bet about?"

"Excuse me?"

"You lost a bet. Over what?"

He let out a soft sigh. "Are you familiar with *Lord of the Rings*?"

"Yes."

"Well in the book there's a character named Merry."

"Yeah ... Merry Brandybuck."

His head jerked back. "How do you know that?"

"Trivia ... go on."

"Apparently, he was originally named Marmaduke. Tolkien changed the name right before the final release of the book."

"And you didn't know that?"

"Nope." There was a pained expression on his face. "Did you?"

"Yes, I'm a beast at pop culture trivia night. Always in the top three."

"Wait, you knew his name was originally Marmaduke Brandybuck?"

"Yes, it's a horrible name but Merry isn't that much better."

"So you're into *Lord of the Rings*?"

"No, I hate those movies. But my brother loved all things Tolkien so I was forced to watch them far too many times."

He pulled up my IT ticket on his computer. "Can you explain what's been going on with the laptop?"

"What hasn't been happening? Sticky keys, disappearing files, lost documents, Pacman ghost."

"Pacman ghost?"

"Yeah, those little shadow figures that run across the screen."

"An interface shadow?" His lip puckered, tilting upward.

"I'm not familiar with the technical term. Do you think we could swap this laptop for a new one?"

"Oh yeah sure. Just let me go to the back and pluck a new computer off of the laptop tree."

"Is that what you guys call the stockroom?"

"I'm going to need to run a diagnostic so I can identify the source of the issues. You can leave the laptop with me and I can give you a temporary loaner."

"So you do have a magical laptop tree."

Reaching for his employee ID badge, he gently tapped it against the badge around my neck. "Now you have my contact information."

Working for a tech company like this one came with some awesome features, one of which was Connectability. Each employee badge was coded with your employee information and could include whatever you were willing to share. My badge was encrypted with my name, department, cube location, email address, and office number. I also had it connected to my professional social media profiles. With the tap of my badge, Jamaal granted me access to his information and gained access to mine. We were also now connected virtually on the company app as Codeability Co-peers. A personalized list of your work friends. It was like Facebook but internal for Codeability employees only.

"Now we're codependent." I beamed. Employees called the app Codependent as an inside joke.

Jamaal chuckled. "This way you can just message me directly when you have more details from your supervisor regarding the problems she's experiencing."

"I can definitely do that."

Standing, Jamaal tugged at his trousers until the hem was flush with his shoes. "And if you need anything ... tech related of course, feel free to message me directly. The line at the help desk can get rather long."

"I don't mind waiting."

"I mind." He blinked sheepishly. "I just mean I know Miles can be demanding. So I'll gladly make cube calls so you don't have to interrupt your workday."

"Thank you, Jamaal."

He swept his tongue over his top lip, leaving it moist and dewy. "I'll walk you back to the help desk to check out that loaner."

2

THE CAFETERIA WAS PACKED. IT WAS SUCH AN annoyance when afternoon meetings forced me to take lunch earlier than normal. I liked my routine, and lunch at two o'clock in the afternoon was part of that. After two, the hungry masses thinned out considerably. Sure, the lasagna bake would be gone, but at least peace and quiet was guaranteed. Grabbing a bowl of tomato soup and a grilled cheese with bacon sandwich, I joined my coworker Risha at one of the last remaining empty tables.

"Is it just me or does this place look more and more like a high school cafeteria each day?" I asked.

"You know how it is. Get 'em when they're young, lure them in with air hockey tables and beer bong nights and then work 'em like dogs." Risha shoved a ruffled chip into her mouth.

"Who knew that at thirty-three I'd be the office OG?"

"You are definitely long in the tooth. And looking more and more your age with each passing day."

I waved my friend's remarks off. Risha Patel was one of the first people I met when I joined Codeability four years ago. I'd been lured away from a medical tech firm that was slowly going belly up when it was revealed the CEO was fudging the numbers. During the recruiting process, I was promised my own team of engineers and app developers and a blank check to do as I saw fit.

Codeability was doing amazing things and I got to be in the

room where the magic happened. My team was responsible for app innovation. Every company needed an app and Codeability was the place those companies went to when they wanted a functional, user-friendly application that kept visitors engaged. It was my job to come up with the newest widgets that would entice the end user to sink hours of time online.

"I noticed your girlfriend came in the other day."

"Don't call her that." I shot her an annoyed glare. I made the mistake a few months back asking Risha a general question about the new hire in executive. Risha quickly deducted two plus two equaled a crush and she never missed an opportunity to tease me about it.

"Laurel at the helpdesk said that when your *little friend* comes in she always asks for you. Does she know you're not the IT troubleshoot guy?"

"Not exactly." Cutting my grilled cheese into small squares, I dipped the toasted bread into my soup bowl.

One week while much of the IT staff was attending a conference, I volunteered to man the helpdesk. Winnie Chambers, with executive, walked in needing IT support and for the next thirty minutes, I bumbled my way through fixing her boss's glitchy computer while trying not to stare too hard at her long legs and heart-shaped mouth. From that interaction, she rightly assumed I was the man to call on when she couldn't log in or her screen froze. For someone who worked at a tech firm, she wasn't really tech savvy.

The thing about Codeability is the owner, Miles Graves, despised titles. Everyone was a valuable part of the team. Instead of titles, we were all considered team partners. Risha Patel, IT team partner. Harry Flick, accounting team partner. This included the CEO all the way down to the cafeteria staff. So to anyone outside of my department, I wasn't the Director of Application Development. I was just Jamaal Singleton, Information Technology team partner.

"Why don't you just ask her out already?"

"How would I do that exactly? Sorry to hear you're having connectivity issues, but I was hoping we could connect on a personal level."

Risha wrinkled her nose. "Not that. Definitely don't say shit like that."

"Beyond an occasional malware sweep, she doesn't even know I exist."

"I know women and she is definitely feeling you."

"You've never even met her."

"Who makes the trip down to the dungeon when they could just submit an IT ticket online? Trust me she isn't interested in tech support."

Risha thought everyone was flirting with me. She'd made it her mission to help me find a mate even though I was perfectly capable of navigating the dating scene on my own. Between Risha and my mother, I had the dating market covered. Risha was hitting up the young eligible women in her circle and my mother was working the other angle, searching for families with beautiful, smart daughters with good heads on their shoulders.

Spooning a hearty serving of soup into my mouth, I scanned the food court and the early bird crowd. Whatever you wanted you could find here, wood-fired pizza, a made-to-order sandwich, carved turkey or brisket ... Winnie. Winnie Chambers was at the salad bar, loading her container with fixings. I instinctually checked my watch, making note of the time. *Was this when she normally took her lunch?*

In the past three months, I'd only seen her in the food court once before. A Winnie sighting was like discovering a red panda in the wild. The encounter left you in awe and marveling at the majesty of God. I was often stuck in the basement, so the comings and goings topside passed me by. And I didn't have much reason to frequent the executive floor. When I did, I always felt like an outsider who took a wrong turn at the water fountain. *Go back to your fiber optic cavern you freak.* Maybe I owed Ryan my gratitude for scheduling a meeting late in the afternoon because if he hadn't, I wouldn't have the pleasure of seeing Miss Chambers.

Miss Chambers, a point she made very clear a few days ago. But just because she wasn't married didn't mean she wasn't with someone. Women like her were rarely ever single. Winnie was a natural beauty. Her mahogany skin was sprinkled with freckles across the bridge of her nose, spilling over to her cheeks. Her style made it clear she didn't track trends, instead wearing clothes that showcased her unique sense of character. Every day she wore brightly colored pants with flowers, polka dots, or geometric zig zags all over them. Those pants hugged her curves and accented her ass which poked out, defying the laws of physics.

Then there was her smile. It was her smile that initially caught my attention. I was the presenter for a cybersecurity training for new hires. Winnie was four rows up and eight seats in at the Gates Learning Annex. I told a lame tech joke and Winnie laughed the hardest and continued to smile long after everyone else had moved on. So clearly, she possessed an amazing sense of humor to go along with that smile. When the class was over, I was left with the memory of her kilowatt grin.

"Are you listening to me?" Risha's voice interrupted my thoughts.

"Yes, I heard every word you said."

"So ... what should I do?"

I swallowed hard. "Follow your heart."

Risha threw her crumpled up napkin at my head. "You weren't listening."

"You're right. But I'm listening now." My ears were listening to Risha, but my eyes were trained on Winnie as she disappeared up the escalator.

> Codeability Co-peer, Jamaal: The computer is all fixed. I can bring it to you if you're available?

Codeability Co-peer, Winnie: That was fast. ☺

> Codeability Co-peer, Jamaal: It was an easy fix. Is now a good time to stop by?

Codeability Co-peer, Winnie: Yes.

After picking up the laptop from the IT service tech that fixed the problem, I headed for the top floor. Each floor of the four-story main building had a different vibe. The fourth floor was reserved for the company's top executives and their support staff with expansive conference rooms, a kitchen, and personal chef that cooked Miles's eggs over easy every morning. Whenever Miles was in the office, the staff was all a buzz. Miles Graves was akin to a rockstar. He had a laid back personality and pretended not to take himself too seriously. But if you asked me, he was acutely aware of the role he played and how he was perceived.

When you exited the elevators, you were greeted by large screens that pumped out company propaganda videos about our vision and mission statements. Codeability was a tech company, we weren't curing cancer. The work was important but Miles Graves wanted you to believe what we were doing was revolutionary. I think that was just baked into any start-up culture. These companies wanted the staff to feel united under a common purpose.

Before heading to Winifred's desk, I made a pit stop in the executive kitchen. All the staff kitchens in the building were stocked with sweet and savory snack items. Oatmeal, a variety of fruit, cereal, candy, chips, granola bars, and drinks. But this kitchen had something the others did not, sweet treats made by Miss Chambers. Every Friday she brought in homemade cookies, pastries, or cupcakes. She'd present the treat in a metal tin with a Post-it Note on top that read *Treat of the Week* followed by a description of what was inside. Today it was salted caramel chocolate bark with candied bacon bits. Removing the lid, I was happy to find a few pieces left. I snagged one, taking a bite.

It was the perfect mouthful of sweet and salty goodness. Every item she'd shared was delicious but I think this was my favorite. Pulling the pen from my pocket, I leaned in to write a quick note on the Post-it.

YOU OUTDID YOURSELF. BEST TREAT YET! THANK YOU FOR MAKING FRIDAY A LITTLE BRIGHTER.

Popping the rest of the candy in my mouth, I turned the corner and made my way through the space. Winnie noticed me straight away as if she'd been eagerly awaiting my arrival. Her face illuminated as if being backlit by an unseen energy force. When I say this, I am not exaggerating. Winnie's smile radiated, causing my heart to jackhammer in my chest and my knees to feel drunk and woozy. *She must be really excited to get this damn laptop back.*

"Hi." She was still beaming.

"Hi." I thrust the computer forward. "Laptop." I frantically scanned her desk looking for something to comment on. "Your desk is ... fun." Her desk was a fire hazard. Stacks of file folders and random envelopes. And then there was the obscene amount of company merch.

"If you ever want a mug or tumbler, just let me know."

"Is that a Miles bobble head?"

"Yeah, Jerrika gave it to me my first week here. She said it was rare merch and she's right. I've only seen one other person with it."

I glanced over at Miles's office. He was on the phone pretending to look important. "FYI he hates that bobblehead."

"What?" Her eyebrows knitted together.

"Yeah it was a promotional thing, but when the dolls came in he fumed because they didn't capture his likeness."

Winnie opened a drawer and swept the bobblehead inside.

"Thank you so much for the laptop and intel. You're a lifesaver."

"Yep." I want to tell you I took a seat and waxed poetic until she had no choice but to beg me to fuck her. But that isn't what happened. Making a quick about face, I retraced my steps back to the elevator bank. As the doors closed to return me to the basement, I cursed myself under my breath. "Fucking idiot."

***

Working in the basement had its perks. No one ever came down here unless they needed something. Because we were tucked away, we were free from micromanagement. And IT threw the best office parties. No drama, just good people, strong drinks, and tech jokes. *Why do they call it hypertext? Because it has too much JAVA. Get it JAVA. Fuck you, that joke kills every time.*

The basement also had its cons. When something important was happening, IT staff was usually the last to know. Big outta sight, outta mind vibes. Also the lack of windows made time indistinguishable. I can't tell you how often I emerged from the basement to be greeted by the moon. This particular afternoon, I managed to log off early and found the sun hidden behind rain-filled clouds that poured from the sky in steady sheets. Searching through my backpack for my umbrella, I exited the building, nearly walking into Winnie who was pacing back and forth underneath the rain shelter.

I grabbed hold of her arm to ensure her stumble didn't end up in a fall. We'd never physically come in contact before, aside from the few times her hand brushed mine when passing an object. "I'm so sorry I didn't see you there."

"I should probably stay out of the way of quitting time traffic."

"It's fine ... seeing you even if it's during a head on collision is always a nice surprise."

"You did almost bowl me over." She giggled.

"I'm stronger than I look."

"You look pretty strong to me." Her eyes pinged from my chest to my arms.

"I like to run." I caught myself stupidly flexing a muscle and hoped she didn't notice. Luckily she was preoccupied by the rain.

"Is everything okay?"

"Yeah, it's raining."

"Don't tell me you melt when you come in contact with water like Evillene?"

"Who?" Her eyebrows mashed together in a frown.

"Evillene from *The Wiz*."

"I've never seen that movie."

"Wait, you know who Merry Brandybucks is but not Evillene?"

She ignored my outrage. "I thought it never rained in Southern California."

"Oh yeah, that song is hella misleading. It should have an asterisk or probably be titled 'It hardly rains in Southern California.' But that's not nearly as catchy."

"So today is one of those asterisk days."

"Yep, I guess so."

She looked off into the distance at the unrelenting rain. "How long do you think it will last?"

I tilted my head to the sky like I was my grandmother who could predict the weather based on her aching joints. "There's no telling. Why?"

"I forgot my umbrella in my car and at this rate I'll be soaked by the time I make it there. I'm meeting a friend for dinner and I don't want to arrive looking like a drowned cat."

"Yeah, that would definitely kill date night."

"Not a date." She rigorously shook her head.

I was thankful she made the distinction. It saved me from obsessing over the woman of my dreams on a date with someone who wasn't me for the rest of the night. Don't get me wrong, I would still think about her tonight and the thoughts would be wholly inappropriate with Winnie in lingerie barely covering her ass.

"I can walk you to your car."

"Really?"

"I'm headed that way anyway." I deployed my umbrella. Winnie dipped her head and joined me underneath. She was so close the fragrance of the peach and amber in her long braids tickled my nostrils. We took off toward the parking lot on the west end of campus. "How are you liking it at Codeability?" Maybe during this short walk I could get to know her better.

"It's nice. Everyone is really nice … for the most part."

"What about Miles, is he really demanding?"

"Umm … I don't think he's ever talked to me actually."

My face crumpled into a frown. "You're his assistant."

"No, I'm his assistant's assistant and Jerrika kind of keeps me busy with coffee runs."

"That sucks."

"It's not all bad. I'm still learning a ton."

"Like?"

"Well … yesterday Miles held a meeting discussing satisfying market demand. I wasn't invited to the meeting but I could hear it from my desk. He speaks really loud. It was like being at a Ted talk."

"Well I'm sure that will be useful one day … eventually."

Her brown eyes slammed into me. "Are you making fun of me?"

"No. Well maybe a little bit."

"Listen, we can't all be IT support professionals like you."

Concern rippled the muscles in my jaw. "Who's making fun now?" I playfully nudged her arm with mine.

"I wasn't. You've saved my tail on several occasions. I tell everybody … go to Jamaal the IT guy, he'll fix you right up."

Risha was right. I really needed to come clean and let her know

I wasn't part of the helpdesk. The only reason I hadn't spoken up sooner was because I looked forward to her surprise visits. Once she knew, she wouldn't have a reason to stop by or ask me for help with her basic IT problems.

"Is that why I have over two hundred urgent emails?"

"Job security."

"Thanks for speaking so highly of me."

"I talk about you all the time." Her eyes grew wide. "No ... not all the time." Her voice rang like a bell in a nervous chuckle.

Clearing my throat, I asked, "I can't imagine you went to school to be the assistant to the assistant."

"No, I went to college for marketing, primarily social media and event planning."

"And now you work here."

"You sound like my parents."

"How so?"

"When I told them I'd landed a job at a Fortune 500 company, they were shocked. When I told them I'd essentially be a gofer, it just confirmed their beliefs about corporate America draining the creativity out of individuals and transforming them into mindless drones."

"We all have to start somewhere."

She smiled. "That's exactly what I said. Working at Codeability allows me to network and build strong connections. Plus, in my role as executive liaison—"

"That's a great title."

"I know right. As an executive liaison I do get to plan events and create flyers."

"So it sounds like you have it all figured out."

"What about you? Working in IT must present all types of opportunities."

"Yeah I have a plan. Ultimately I hope to be my own boss one day."

"Ooo, and then you could hire me and I could be your social media guru."

"I'd hire you in a heartbeat. I mean we'd definitely have to sign you up for some beginner computer literacy training ... but still."

"Whoa, shots fired."

"You submitted an IT ticket for a battery issue only to discover the power cord was loose."

"In my defense, that wasn't immediately obvious."

"It's the first thing you check."

"Maybe if you have an IT background."

"It's kind of common sense."

"Are you implying I lack common sense?"

I expelled a deep breath. "Umm ...psst. Never that."

Winnie pointed to a white Mazda. "This is me." She used her key fob to unlock the doors. "Thanks so much for sharing your umbrella."

"Any time. If you need an umbrella, an ergonomic mouse, or a kidney you know where to find me."

"Don't you have to be my match to donate an organ?"

"Who says I'm not?"

Winnie's smile was a whisper. *This would be the perfect time to ask her out. Do you want to hang out sometime? Maybe we could grab a bite one of these days? What's your thoughts on deep dish pizza because I know this place that is almost as good as Chicago.*

"Drive safe," I said. Any plans I had for tonight would have to be cancelled because I would be replaying the last few minutes of this conversation over and over again in my head, trying to determine where I went wrong.

"You too."

I waited for her to pull off, offering a wave. Once Winnie's car was out of sight, I turned around and walked back the way I'd just came. Winnie was parked on the west side of campus while I was parked on the east side. Did I just walk ten minutes out of my way to spend time with her? Yes. Would I do it again? Absolutely.

3

I HATED THE LOWE CONFERENCE ROOM. IT WAS WAY across campus and this building gave me the heebie-jeebies because it reminded me of something out of a horror movie. While walking the halls, I almost expected to bump into a ghost. In less than an hour, Miles Graves and his design team would be in this room and I was in charge of ensuring everything was set up from food to audio visual. The food I had covered. A long table in the corner of the room was laid out with snack items and drinks for the afternoon meeting.

However, the audio visual was not going as smoothly. The projector wouldn't connect to the laptop. I restarted the computer and unplugged the connectors and pushed every foreign button on the projector remote. At one point I just stood there with my hands on my hips trying to mentally will the equipment to do my bidding. The extent of my IT expertise had been exhausted. But luckily, I knew a guy.

Codeability Co-peer, Winnie: I need you.

Codeability Co-peer, Jamaal: …

Codeability Co-peer, Winnie: I'm in the Lowe's conference room and the projector won't work.

Codeability Co-peer, Jamaal: Give me five minutes.

He was there in four, out of breath with beads of sweat dotting his forehead. *Had he run all the way across campus like Olympic track star Malcolm Bishop to help me out?* That was world class customer service.

"What seems to be the problem?"

"Miles has a meeting in less than thirty minutes, and I can't get the damn projector and laptop to sync."

"Let me take a look." He walked toward me with determined steps and my heart fluttered in my chest.

I followed him into the small AV closet in the back of the room. He pulled off his suit jacket to reveal a blue button-up shirt and a gun show. His build was lean and athletic, which could easily be natural or from time spent in the gym. Given a few hours and a thorough examination, I'm sure I could figure it out. Jamaal used the projector remote to pull up the menu.

"What are you doing?" I didn't really care, I just wanted to hear the rumble of his deep voice fill the void.

"Checking the settings. And seeing if I can manually sync the laptop."

Squatting, he examined the mess of cords on the bottom shelf. I lowered myself to my knees so I could observe. His face was serious, and he bit his lower lip while sorting through blue and yellow cords. My eyes were trained on him as he pushed his glasses over the bridge of his nose. I'd always been a sucker for a man with glasses. Some women liked a nice ass or strong legs. I preferred my men, visually impaired.

"Here hold this." He handed me his cell phone with the flashlight on. "Point that straight ahead."

I complied, happy to be hired on as his IT assistant. Jamaal reached for a cord and pulled it from the hard drive bank. In the other room, the projector whirled to a stop. Plugging the cord back in, the gears spun as the projector cycled through the restart process.

"What did you just do?"

"Sometimes the best solution is the easiest one." His voice echoed slightly in the empty space. "How much longer do we have before your meeting starts?"

I glanced at his phone. "Twenty minutes." My voice trembled, revealing the anxiousness I was attempting to conceal.

"It takes about ten minutes for the system to fully restart." Jamaal lowered himself on to the carpet. "So now we wait."

"I really can't thank you enough for this."

"Don't thank me yet, Winifred."

I wrinkled my nose at his formal name choice. "Winnie."

"Do you not like being called Winifred?"

"No it's not that. My friends and family all call me Winnie. When I hear the name Winifred it feels like I'm in trouble." Hopefully he wanted to be one of my friends. I was a good listener, trustworthy, and funny. "Are you originally from San Diego?"

"Yeah, I'm the guy who never left his city."

"San Diego isn't a bad place to be stuck in. You should see some of the towns I've visited."

"Military brat?"

"Nope, I grew up in a traveling circus so I'm from everywhere."

Jamaal leaned in closer, my words catching him by surprise. "Are you shitting me right now?"

"Nope, it's called The Howling Bazaar." I howled low and deep.

Jamaal's face was frozen in disbelief. "I need to know all the details."

I glanced at my phone checking the time. "My father was a carney, part of Chambers and Sons. They were tumblers, twisters. Their bodies could contort in freakishly weird ways. My mom was a gymnast in college. And one night she attended a show and was impressed with my dad's performance. So much so that a week later she left with him."

"Your mom dropped out of college to follow a circus performer?"

"Haven't you ever felt the spontaneous urge to go left when everyone else is traveling right?"

"I like knowing what's up ahead … so no. What did your mother say to her parents?"

"She told them she was in love and was going to marry Rocko Chambers."

Jamaal's facial expression was incredulous. "But what if that shit all went horribly wrong?"

"So it's true what they say about tech people?"

"What's that?"

"All widgets and statistical odds, no time for wonder."

"Okay, nobody says that. You can't tell me you'd just run off with a guy you barely knew."

"Not just for any old guy but for the right guy, yes. My mother claimed their souls met before. And when she ran away with him, everything started to make sense."

"And they're still together?"

"Thirty-five years and counting. I know it's crazy. I've never really been in love so I don't entirely understand it myself."

"Wait, you've never been in love? I find that hard to believe."

"Okay, let me restate. I've been in love but it's not the same type of love Whitney and Mary J. were singing about."

"Ahh … you mean that I can't breathe without you type of love."

"Yeah I've never relied on a man for my oxygen supply." It would appear fate was providing me with an opening, so I took it. "What about you, are you currently crazy in love with someone?" I studied his face intently, awaiting a reply. *Please say no. Please say no.*

"Uh, not for quite some time."

It took all my effort to force back the smile that was curving the corners of my mouth. "Oh, that's a shame."

Like magic, the presentation on the laptop was now on full display on the screen in the main room, illuminating the space. Unable to contain my excitement, I flung my arms around Jamaal, giving him a tight hug. He felt solid and strong like he could lift my ass up with very little effort. Jamaal's hand landed on my back and the accelerated beats of my heart drowned out everything else around me.

Pulling away, I jumped to my feet. "Thank you."

Jamaal rose from the floor and stared down at me. "Glad I could be useful."

"You're very helpful. I mean I bet there's all types of things you could do that I'd appreciate."

Jamaal blinked rapidly, never taking his eyes off my face. "Well, if you come up with any other things that need doing, just give me a call."

Heat trickled up the back of my neck. He had no idea what he was suggesting. The things that I would do to him would leave us both blushing.

Jamaal cleared his throat. "Winnie, I was thinking maybe you would want—" He was interrupted by a gaggle of people entering the conference room. The meeting was set to start any minute.

"Looks like it's showtime. Thanks for the last-minute rescue."

He rubbed the back of his neck. "Yeah, I'll get out of your hair."

"Hopefully I'll see you around."

"You bet."

I was in the final meeting of the day and beyond ready to go home. As executive liaison, part of my job responsibilities were to execute Miles's focus on building a sense of community among the staff.

Once a month, we hosted an event to boost team morale. This Friday Miles himself would be speaking. Jerrika and I were finalizing details along with members from the social media team.

"So Miles should speak for about fifteen minutes or so and then right after we'll direct everyone to the north lawn for food, drinks, and live entertainment," I said, running through the simple agenda to ensure everyone was on the same page.

"Will Miles be sticking around for the festivities?" Maurice, a member of the social media team, asked.

Jerrika puckered her lips. "Miles is super busy, he has a flight to catch so I doubt he'll be able to enjoy the tacos and refried beans."

I cleared my throat, chiming in. "His flight doesn't leave until ten. I know it would mean a lot to the staff if he hung out for a bit. Giving employees an opportunity to chat with him if only for an hour would be great. It would go a long way to make people feel listened to."

"Miles is unavailable." Jerrika's tone was harsh, but I wasn't easily deterred.

I scrolled through his calendar on my company tablet. "The event starts at five. Miles is slated to speak at five fifteen. He has an interview scheduled at six. So there is a window of time in between even if it's just for thirty minutes," I offered.

Jerrika flashed me an evil eye. She didn't appreciate me speaking up in these meetings. Something about undermining her authority. Which she had very little of. Jerrika was the type of boss who micromanaged everything I did while providing absolutely no guidance. She liked adding in her two cents, but oftentimes her contributions were tone deaf.

I was new so I was doing my best to feel her out while trying to assert my boundaries, but it was a delicate balancing act. I'd learned the importance of picking my battles and this wasn't one I was looking to go to war over, so I let it go. Almost.

"I've listened to a lot of employees express their views on Codeability and its CEO and time and time again, I've heard the same complaint. Miles is more of an enigma than a real person. Maybe this Friday won't work, but we should look for ways to allow Miles to connect with the staff so he feels relatable."

I was sitting in a room with event planning and social media marketing, two teams I would love to be a part of. I wasn't trying to overstep, but I also wanted to show I was more than just a meeting scribe.

"What exactly did you have in mind?" Maurice asked.

Jerrika let out a nervous chuckle. "Maybe we should table this discussion for a later date."

"Just looking to hear some new perspectives." Maurice pointed in my direction. "Go on."

"It could be something as simple as lunch time chats. Meals with Miles in which we select ten or twenty employees once a month who have lunch with Miles. A chance for an intimate conversation. Employees get to hear about the company's vision from the horse's mouth and he gets to gauge the temperature of his workforce."

"Miles would never go for that," Jerrika insisted.

As his personal assistant, she also considered herself the gate-keeper of admission. But she was more like a cock blocker. If she didn't like you, she would limit your access. I don't know what Ramsey from Human Resources had done, but he'd been trying to get a meeting on the calendar with Miles since I'd started here. Each time I placed him on the calendar, Jerrika would cancel the meeting siting scheduling conflicts.

"I don't know, maybe if we asked he might surprise you."

Jerrika slammed her laptop shut. "Winnie, I think this meeting is just about over. Why don't you head back to your desk and type up the notes."

And with those words, I was banished from the conference room. Sinking into my chair back at my desk, I had to admit this was not how I'd pictured my Codeability experience. I knew I would have to fetch coffee and stuff envelopes, but I also hoped I'd be able to sit in on meetings and offer my input without being shut down like I was a child.

But every day I put on a smile and tried my best to make a good impression. You never knew who was watching and so I worked hard regardless of the task. If you needed me to blow up five hundred balloons to create a balloon arch, it would be the best helium filled arch ever crafted. When I was fulfilling lunch orders, I always made sure to include a cookie or piece of chocolate. Because who doesn't like a sweet treat after a meal?

I never expected this to be easy and everyone had to start somewhere. Even Miles Graves was just an intern at a small tech firm before he was Miles Graves, the man on the cover of *Forbes* magazine and one of the richest self-made millionaires. And he was quickly chasing the billionaire status which was an impressive feat for a Black kid from California.

So yes, I would tolerate Jerrika's poor management style and lack of people skills. I would collate, prepare PowerPoints, and field calls because I truly believed hard work gets rewarded. Maybe I'm a little naive but it couldn't all be nepotism and the old boys club. People like me managed to break through in the past and that was all the motivation I needed.

It was nine o'clock at night and with Law and Order SVU, my emotional support TV show, playing in the background, I was mixing batter for my butter pecan cupcakes. The apartment door opened and Simone, my roommate, came bounding in. I met Simone Vance five months ago. She had a vacant room and I needed a place to stay. Luckily for me, we hit it off immediately and she was quickly becoming a new best friend.

"How was your date?" I asked.

"It's a one and done. He didn't ask me a single question about myself and he made me split the bill."

I cringed. "Is this what I have to look forward to?"

"Yes, the dating scene in San Diego is abysmal." She tossed her purse on the couch and removed her high heels.

"Well at least you looked cute."

"What are you doing?" She eyed the mess of bowls and measuring spoons on the kitchen counter.

"Making cupcakes." I offered her the batter-coated spatula.

"It's Tuesday."

She was correct, normally Thursday nights were reserved for baking but tonight I was making an exception. "Yes, I'm making a special batch of treats for the IT guy. He helped me out today and I wanted to show my appreciation."

"You need to stop lusting after the IT guy and find a real man." She gave her hands a quick wash in the kitchen sink.

"Jamaal is real. He's smart, handsome, and unlike your date tonight, he asks questions."

"Rude." She tossed a rubber trivet at me. "Sounds like he's the perfect guy. You should ask him out."

I released a nervous chuckle. "No ... I couldn't."

"Winnie, we are living in a time where women can do whatever they want. Including asking a guy out on a date." Simone used her index finger to collect batter from the spatula before licking it clean.

I'd never asked anyone on a date. I just flirted until they eventually got the hint. Needless to say I didn't get asked out very often. Probably because my idea of flirting was asking questions like ... "If civilization collapsed and you were one of a handful of survivors, what's your special skill to help rebuild the world?" Because I know you're curious, mine is optimism. People are in desperate need of that in their darkest moments.

I didn't have a traditional childhood social experience. No homecoming, no prom. No lusting after my crush when he walked past me in the hall. My friends were the children who traveled and performed with their parents. Most of them were more like extended family, not potential love connections. My first boyfriend was the son of a fire eater.

"That's what the cupcakes are for."

"So you think he's going to eat those cupcakes and then want to eat you?"

My cheeks flushed with heat. God I could only hope so. Don't get me wrong, I didn't just want to sleep with Jamaal. Although that was a top priority. I also wanted to get to know everything about him and win over his heart and make him fall madly in love with me.

"I read somewhere men love to be asked out. It takes the pressure off of them and they find it sexy as hell."

I was the woman who went off to college and started dating the first man who showed me any attention. All our friends joked Tyler and I were going to end up married. The thought terrified me. Which is probably why I cheated on him senior year, effectively ending any chance at a future.

"I'm not as courageous as you."

"You're in a new city, with new opportunities. This is the perfect time to reinvent yourself. Instead of being shy, reserved Winnie Chambers, be the woman who asks for what she wants."

"Even when the answer could be no?"

"Especially then." Simone poured herself a tall glass of wine and headed to her bedroom with the spatula.

Maybe she was right. I was reminded of the saying, "A life well lived depends on one's courage." It was time for my crush on Jamaal to transition from pining to dry humping and end in naked twister. If the past few months had taught me anything, it was that I was capable of being a strong, independent woman. I'd moved away from everyone and everything I knew to plant roots in a new city. After a brief search, I landed a job at a coveted company. And I found this sweet apartment with my own room and a bed that wasn't a pull out. On the circus circuit, we traveled in an RV. My siblings and I had pull-down bunk beds with only a curtain providing privacy.

After college, I rejoined my family on the road, hoping to land a gig as the social media manager for the circus. But I quickly learned I wasn't the same person and my family was no longer the center of my universe. I'd taken a big risk moving back to California with no friends, no family, and no clue. If I could do all that, surely I could muster up the steel to ask an attractive man out for coffee. I was Winnie Chambers of the Catapulting Chambers, and we always landed on our feet.

4

WHEN I GOT TO MY DESK ON WEDNESDAY MORNING, I was greeted by a yellow metal container that said "Made with love, always fresh" on the lid. I surveyed desks nearby and mine was the only one with this addition. Dropping my bag in my chair, I reached for the note card.

JAMAAL,
JUST WANTED TO SAY THANK YOU ONCE AGAIN FOR ALL
YOUR HELP YESTERDAY AND EVERY DAY.
WITH GRATITUDE,
WINNIE

The corners of my mouth crept up into a smile.

Risha poked her head over the cubicle. "Do you have a secret admirer?"

"Hardly."

Rounding the corner, Risha snatched the card from my hand, reading it with a smirk. "If this isn't an invitation to fuck I don't know what is."

I looked around the room, making sure employees powering up their computers hadn't overheard. "Could you please keep your voice down?"

"Sorry lover boy, I didn't mean to embarrass you." She plopped herself onto my desk. "What's in the box?"

I lifted the lid, revealing beautifully decorated cupcakes. The tops were adorned with tiny candy keyboards.

"She likes you."

"She's just being nice. I helped her out yesterday."

"A woman doesn't spend her time off making cupcakes with hand crafted details to be nice. She could have bought you a box of cupcakes from the grocery store. But no ... she went out of her way to let you know you could get it on-site."

"Get what exactly?"

"Do I really need to explain the birds and the bees to you?" She narrowed her eyes.

"No thank you. I would prefer it if you didn't." Risha reached for a cupcake and I lightly slapped her hand. "Excuse you."

"What? You're not going to eat all these cupcakes by yourself."

Selecting a cupcake, I handed it to her. "Now go away. It's far too early for your shit."

Risha hopped down from my desk, leaving me with a few parting words. "The ball is in your court. Hope you don't choke."

Pushing the tin box aside, I logged into my computer. In many cultures, food was considered a love language. Maybe Risha wasn't off track. What if this was Winnie's way of testing the waters to see if I'd bite? The fact that she left work and baked me a sweet confection did mean she was thinking about me last night while in the comfort of her home, probably wearing little to nothing.

Which oddly enough is exactly how I dreamt about her in the early hours of the morning. Whipped cream covered her naughty bits and she was taunting me to lick her clean. As my face inched closer to her creamy center, my alarm went off and ripped me from my happy ending. I woke up disoriented with my dick on hard. So I did what I always did when Winnie came to mind. I beat my meat with the thought of her writhing in ecstacy underneath me.

After knocking out a portion of code for a large project, I

decided to grab a drink. The food court downstairs had decent coffee but the Bean There Done That across campus was superior and since the weather was nice, I opted to go for a walk. I loved the Codeability campus. It was a little village with everything one could possibly need. When the weather was warm and cool like it was now—and honestly this was San Diego, the weather was almost always amazing—I'd bike to work.

I'd aspired to work at a place like this since junior high school. Truthfully, I thought the company, the tech, and the staff would all be mine. One of my prized possessions was a notebook filled with prospective start-up business ideas. Codeability was my dream ... but it was too nice of a day to get into all of that. I passed the gaming nook, which was a deceptive name because it was a two story building with rooms for single and multiplayer game play. The first floor housed old school arcade machines and foosball and pool tables. Upstairs there were game tables and every board game ever created. Yes, I'd partaken in a game night or two with coworkers playing the epic strategy game Rising Sun.

I was in no rush to head back to my cube, so my stride was leisurely but someone from behind was gaining on me at a rapid pace. Moving to the left, I tried to allow them enough room to pass. The approaching footsteps quickened and were followed by a salutation.

"Hi," Winnie said, gasping for breath.

"You good?" Her accelerated rate of breathing was cause for concern.

"Oh ... me? Yeah. I just never run and in recent months I've been living off of Twinkie's and pizza because of work. Couple that with my asthma and here we are."

"You might want to check that out though because it doesn't sound normal," I teased.

"Shut up, I just need a minute."

I matched her slowed tempo so she could steady her breathing. "Why were you in such a hurry?"

"What?" Her braided bun had shifted to the left slightly.

"You were running. I assume you have somewhere important to be."

"No. I just saw you and wanted to say hi."

I could feel heat spread over my mahogany skin. *She'd run all the way over here just to say hello to me?* Asthma be damned.

"Thank you for the cupcakes by the way. You didn't have to go to all the trouble."

"It wasn't any trouble. I love to bake. Every Friday I bring in a new sweet treat. If you're ever in the executive kitchen you should snag a bite."

"Way ahead of you. I look forward to Friday's because I know your special desserts will be waiting for me." *The thought of you is the highlight of my day.*

"I'm happy to hear you're a fan."

"That chocolate bark with the candied bacon was the best thing I've put in my mouth in ages." *I'm not trying to be presumptuous, but I imagine the only thing that could top it would be me sinking my tongue into your honeypot.*

"I have all types of treats I'm sure you'd like."

"I believe you." *I have treats too long, thick, crème filled.*

"Where are you headed?"

"Coffee break." *God the way she looked up at me with those doe-like eyes.*

"My favorite café drink is coffee soda."

That sounds disgusting. "Never heard of it."

"It's cold brew and soda water." She wagged her finger at me. "Don't wrinkle your face up like that, it's delicious."

"I'll take your word for it."

"Don't take my word. Next coffee run is on me."

Was she trying to woo me with caffeinated beverages? Grabbing coffee together was great but I needed more than a thirty-minute link up. I wanted time to get to know her and see her outside of her work clothes. The door was never going to be more open than it was right now. Ask her out.

"The other day you mentioned you'd never seen *The Wiz*?"

Winnie flashed me a shifty eye. "Is this the part where you ask for my Black card? Because it's been suspended, and renewal is currently under review."

"No, I'm not looking to pull your card. Although I'm glad to hear the authorities are investigating the matter," I joked. "How are you the reigning trivia champion if you haven't seen that movie?"

"I've watched *The Wizard of Oz*. It's pretty much the same thing."

Stopping in my tracks, I admonished her. "See and that's exactly why your card was revoked."

"Very funny." She playfully nudged me, letting her hand linger on my arm for longer than expected. Her touch made my skin pebble with goose pimples.

"It is absolutely, positively, not even remotely the same movie." I shook my head from side to side. "This cannot stand. I will not let you go another year without the pleasure of watching the visual and musical extravaganza that is *The Wiz*. Diana Ross, Michael Jackson, Nipsey Russell, Richard Pryor—"

"I'm aware of the cast. Thank you."

"This insanity needs to end." I pulled out my phone. "When are you free?"

"For what?"

"You, me, and the Wizard."

"Like a watch party?" The light breeze ruffled the hem of her skirt.

No, like a date. God Jamaal just ask her out already. "Umm ... yeah. I mean I guess you could call it that." My stomach performed a somersault, and I was ready to abort this mission.

"Yeah sure." Her big mink eyes were speaking to me, in them

lied a hint of excitement, a touch of wonderment, and a dollop of surprise.

"How about tonight?" *Too aggressive.* I bit into the side of my cheek. Nonchalant didn't exist in my vocabulary. I was the guy that texted you right after a date to tell you I had an amazing time. The next day I would call and ask you out on another date because I couldn't wait to see you again. On the second date I was scheduling the third. Some women though find my approach as too eager. But if you liked someone shouldn't you be geeked to spend time with them?

"Would it be pathetic of me if I admitted I had absolutely nothing planned for tonight?" Winnie asked.

"Well neither do I, so who am I to judge?"

"I guess we're just two loveless losers."

I narrowed my eyes.

"No, we're not. You're definitely not a loser. I mean you have a great job and those nice shoes."

We both looked down at my shoes. "You can tell I'm a quality person by my shoes?"

"You can tell a lot about a guy based on his shoes."

"I'm interested. What do my shoes say about me?"

She considered my feet for a minute before responding. "I feel confident that a guy like you in that loafer and sock combination is bagging multiple bitches. Like you're probably getting so much rando vag you don't even know what to do with it."

"Really? So my shoes scream womanizer?"

"Uhm ... a little bit, yeah." The bridge of her nose crinkled when she laughed.

"Okay damn, I'm throwing the shoes away."

"No don't do that." She reached for my hand. *Winnie Chambers was holding my hand.*

"They're gone." I moved closer, gazing down at her. "And for the record, I do not entertain rando vag." Winnie stared at me, her perfect pouty lips parted as if words had escaped her.

A phone alarm chimed from her skirt pocket, and all of sudden she was like Cinderella trying to escape the ball. "I need to head back and set up for a meeting."

"Alright. Umm, does seven o'clock tonight work for you? I can come to your place if that's cool?"

"Yes. I'll text you my address."

"Great. After this, I think you can go through the appeals process to get your Black card back," I joked.

"Ahh ... there are just a few other movies I haven't seen."

"Like what?"

"*Friday, Next Friday* ... all the Friday movies. *Dreamgirls, Harlem Nights, Get Out*—"

"Sounds like we have a lot of work to do."

Winnie flashed a huge smile before jogging back the way she came.

5

IN MY BEDROOM, I PULLED YET ANOTHER ITEM FROM MY closet. To show cleavage or not to show cleavage, that was the question. Was this a date or just new friends hanging out? The last thing I wanted to do was put on an outfit that said bend me over and spank me if he was wearing basketball shorts and a wrinkled T-shirt. I couldn't even ask Simone for help because when I told her Jamaal was coming over, she'd hightailed it to her parents' house.

Which was a huge sacrifice because her parents were conservative and would often provoke heated arguments. The last time I'd tagged along for Sunday dinner, her parents went into a diatribe about how she'd turned her back on their faith and they didn't want her to burn in hell for all eternity. Not an easy conversation to have over pot roast, mashed potatoes, and snow peas.

I opted for jeans that hugged my curves just right with a tangerine bodysuit that always garnered compliments because of the way the bright color popped against my sepia skin. My box braids were styled half up half down, allowing a few braids to frame my face. To top the look off, I spritzed on my favorite fragrance gifted to me by my mother for Christmas. Heading to the kitchen, I pulled the snack foods out of the oven and air fryer. Nothing special just wings, mozzarella sticks, flatbread pizza, sliders, fries and an assortment of dipping sauces. What was movie night without finger food?

There was a knock on my door at seven o'clock sharp, which didn't surprise me. This man was meticulous in everything he did. Why would the concept of time be any different? Rushing to the door, I stalled before opening it. I desperately wanted this night to go well and for the man I'd been crushing on to live up to the hype. With a deep exhale, I expelled the nervous energy from my lungs. Swinging the door open, I greeted Jamaal with a huge smile. It was brief, but his eyes grew wide and tripped down the length of my body before he quickly regained his composure, locking in on my face. He was wearing sweatpants and a T-shirt with a cartoon floppy disk on it. This wasn't a date. He was dressed like he was ready to stuff his face with fried foods and obnoxiously talk through the entire movie.

"Hi," he said.

"Glad to see you found the place okay."

"You look different." He gestured in my direction.

"So do you. Sweatpants."

"Oh yeah." He plunged his hands in his pockets and the fabric stretched over his crotch and I could distinctly make out the outline of his dick. *Why was I like this?* Maybe because since moving to San Diego my sex life had stalled. And after several months, the pangs of sexual starvation were setting in. I desperately wanted to break this fast.

"It's fine you look ... comfy," I said, prying my eyes from his nether regions. It was at this point when I realized he was still standing outside. Stepping aside, I allowed him to come in. I was used to seeing Jamaal in button ups, khakis, and ties so seeing him in a relaxed fit was surprising. It's not like I really expected him to show up at my door like he was punching in for an eight-hour shift.

Walking into the living room, his head was on a swivel. "I've passed this apartment complex a hundred times. I didn't know they were so nice inside."

Following him, I agreed, "Yeah, I really lucked out. When I got the job at Codeability, I didn't have a place to live and I came across a posting for a roommate on a social forum site."

"It's nice being so close to work."

"It is. A bit more pricey, but having a roommate helps."

"Where's your roommate now?"

"She's spending the night at her folks' house." Once the words crossed my lips, I was painfully aware of how it all sounded. He was probably thinking I'd made my roommate leave in the hopes we'd end up having loud, sweaty sex.

"Oh." He rubbed his free hand over his short tapered fade.

"She's really close to them and she's like over there all the time." That was a little white lie, but he didn't need to know that.

He lifted his arm, swinging a pack of beers back and forth.

"Great, you brought a sex pack. SIX. A six-pack." I scratched at the back of my neck. "Damn Invisalign. I'm going to go remove these so I'm not slurring my words before I've had my first drink."

I rushed to the bathroom, not waiting for a response to remove the nonexistent retainers. He hadn't even been here for five minutes and I was acting weird. In my imagination, this man had fucked me all over this apartment. Including draping me over the balcony while he hit it from behind. But now that he was no longer a figment of my oversexed imagination, I was having difficulty coping.

Staring at my reflection in the mirror, I chided myself. "Girl, keep it easy and light." It was time to channel my inner cool girl, which was so not on brand for me. I wasn't the cool girl, I was the girl who preferred arts and crafts over sports and died on the first level of every video game I'd ever played. Just trying not to embarrass myself was the best I could hope for.

When I reentered the room, I found Jamaal in the kitchen. "You've been busy." He gestured toward the various platters.

"Oh that's nothing. It was all pre-made. I just had to fry it or pop it in the toaster oven."

"I was going to order us pizza. The last thing I wanted was for you to come home from work and have to clock into the kitchen."

I waved his words off. "It wasn't any trouble really. I love to entertain."

"Well I appreciate it." He tagged me on the shoulder like I was the little homie.

Was I being friend zoned not even ten minutes into our Netflix and chill? This wouldn't be the first time a man settled me into friendship territory. I wasn't like Simone. When she and I walked into a room people noticed her, never me. I was petite and although my driver's license stated I was five six, I was actually two inches shorter.

Somehow I always managed to get lost in the background. Don't get me wrong, I'm not claiming ugly. But there were levels to this beauty shit and I was pretty in a cute little sister type of way. When most men looked at me, they weren't thinking about mind-numbing sex. Maybe it was the freckles or the fact I often dressed like a kindergarten teacher.

"Where's your remote? I'll get everything set up."

"On the tray on the coffee table. While you do that, I'll make you a plate. What do you want to—"

"Everything. I want everything you have to offer." His gaze was intense, like maybe he was referring to more than the buffalo wings and fried cheese.

My throat rippled with a swallow. Why was I such a slut for this man? "A little bit of everything. Roger that."

With plates and beers in hand, we settled in on the couch and were off to see the Wizard. When Diana Ross got sucked into Oz and the first notes of "He's The Wizard" rang out, I was convinced I would never be able to watch the unseasoned version of *The Wizard of Oz* ever again. Don't get me wrong, Judy Garland was that bitch, but *The Wiz* was just so vibrant and real. I glanced at Jamaal whose gaze was fixed on me with a goofy smile anticipating my reaction to each scene.

"What?" I asked.

"I told you it was good."

"Good, this shit is spectacular. Black excellence." I turned back to the television screen as my face and ears grew hot under the weight of Jamaal's scrutinizing eyes. This wasn't a date, but my racing heart and throbbing pussy hadn't received the message. By the time the mean ole lion made an appearance, I'd inched slightly closer to Jamaal and felt his muscular arm brush against mine. At my request, Jamaal rewound so I could sing along poorly with "A Brand New Day." It was a performance complete with hip thrust, smooth spins, and a snake arm dance that Jamaal received and returned. I loved that he indulged my silliness.

As the credits rolled, Jamaal pulled two sheets of paper out of the pocket of his sweats.

"What's this?"

"I always like to rate a movie after watching it. Corny I know, but I've been doing it since I was a kid."

I flipped the sheet of paper over in my hands. He'd created a scorecard for tonight. The quality Kinko's worthy with a cartoon face resembling mine. It was titled Winnie's Wiz Wrap-up. Underneath that was the name of the movie and the year it was released. The chunk of the scorecard was sectioned off into various categories, acting, costume, plot, and favorite scene. Lastly, there was a spot for an overall score.

"You made me a personalized movie scorecard?"

"Yes."

"When did you have time to do this?"

"It took like five minutes."

"Is that supposed to be me?" I point to the drawing of a brown-skinned woman with braids and a bright smile.

"It's just a rough sketch. If I had more time I could've made it more realistic. Captured the freckle placement and the hint of amber in your eyes."

I smiled so wide a cramp formed in my cheeks. He liked me.

He wanted to kiss me. I was going to fuck this man within an inch of his life.

"This is the nicest thing anyone has ever done for me."

"It's nothing."

I reached for his hand and gave it a squeeze. "It's everything. It means everything to me."

Jamaal's gaze took on a faraway quality. It was like he was looking at me while envisioning a future point in time. My eyes focused in on his lips and silently pleaded for him to kiss me.

"Winnie?"

"Yes, Jamaal," I cooed.

He leaned forward and my heart downshifted into a slow beat as I braced for the dizzying impact his lips touching mine would surely cause. Taking a braid in his hand, he stroked my locks between his fingers. This man was a nerd and I wanted him to slide his pen into my pocket protector. "You know what I like the most about you?"

"No, I mean there's so many amazing qualities to choose from," I joked.

He breathed out a laugh. "I like the way I feel when you look at me."

I lowered my voice before speaking. "How do I make you feel?"

Loud banging punctured the moment.

"I tried but my parents are assholes." Simone entered the apartment like a tornado. Keys were tossed toward the hook but missed the mark and fell to the floor with a jingle. Her overnight bag dropped to the carpet as she tried to untangle herself from her purse strap. "I sure hope your night was better than mine. How was your date?"

Jamaal and I sat in silence, staring at Hurricane Simone. When she finally stopped spinning long enough to look in my direction, her jaw unhinged. "I feel like I'm interrupting something," she announced, raking her hands through her hair.

I felt Jamaal's hand land on the side of my thigh. And I didn't even have a chance to process the fact that he was touching me. I needed to clean up the mess Simone had just created.

When I stood Jamaal's hand slipped from my leg. "What are you doing here?"

"I tried to stay away as long as I could but if I had to be in that house any longer, I was going to end up on the local news for murder."

Simone was too wrapped up in whatever transpired with her parents to even recognize the beseeching expression on my face. I was silently willing her to stop talking. I released a long irritated huff. "Simone, this is Jamaal." I pointed to him, hoping acknowledging his presence would bring her back to reality.

Simone smiled wide. "Nice to meet the man who finally convinced Winnie to watch *The Wiz*. I tried to get her to watch it a couple of times but she always had some lame excuse. I guess I wasn't as persuasive as you ... or as handsome."

Standing, Jamaal extended his hand. "Nice to meet you." He shook her hand before turning to me. "It looks like Simone's had a tough evening so maybe it's best if we call it a night."

The pout of my lips was visible.

"No, don't end your night because of me. I'm cool. My parents do this all the time. I'm just going to head to my room, put in my earbuds, and drift off to sleep. You two can be as loud as you need to. Once I'm asleep, I'm essentially dead to the world." Simone collected her things and grabbed a brownie, mouthing the words "My bad" on her way out.

"I'm sorry about ... all of that."

"No need to apologize. Shit happens. I enjoyed spending time with you."

"So the night is over?"

"Well there are a ton of movies you haven't seen so we should definitely plan to do this again. And when it's all done you can have them call me as a witness. I'm willing to testify on your behalf regarding your rehabilitation and all the reasons your Black card should no longer be denied."

"You'd do that for me," I played into his joke with exaggerated googly eyes.

"I'd do practically anything for you."

My insides liquefied and I released a soft moan that I hoped was undetectable.

Jamaal captured my hand in his. His touch caused me to spiral. My head was light and my breathing labored. His thumb stroked the palm of my hand. Who knew an innocent touch could push me to the edge? *Kiss me you coward.*

"Have a good night." He dropped my hand and headed out the door.

I was left in the entry hall painfully aware of the hot pulsating throb of my lady parts, which would only be satiated by my trusty and overworked rose shaped toy. Well, that was anticlimactic. I'd hoped for a kiss that devolved into sex on the carpet. Grabbing a brownie, I took a huge bite. Why couldn't Simone have shown up fifteen minutes later? Allowing time for a kiss and a quick make-out session. A knock on the door almost made me choke on my treat. Checking the peephole, Jamaal was on the other side. I chewed the remaining blondie brownie and swept my tongue over my teeth to ensure there was nothing caught in them before opening the door.

"Did you forget something?"

He flashed a nervous smile. "I've been watching a ton of self-actualization videos and one of the main themes is that words mean things. So we should choose our words with intention. You know ... saying what we feel in the moment and not missing opportunities to advocate for the things we want. So, I don't want to hang out again—"

"Wow, you came all the way back here to tell me to kick rocks? This is new." It appeared Simone was correct. The dating scene was a swamp.

"Wait no ... absolutely not. I came back to ask you on a date."

I released the built up tension in my shoulders and back. "I'd thought you'd never ask."

"I also wanted to kiss you goodnight. But then I got all into my head and started second guessing myself. It's a bad habit' I'm always weighing the pros and cons. But I'm working on living in the moment and being more—"

Fuck it. Grabbing his face, I kissed him. I loved the sound of his voice, but I was in need of physical nonverbal communication. Jamaal's lips were pillows and when he brushed his tongue over my mouth, it was as if he was asking for permission to take this deeper. I parted my lips slightly, granting him access, and he slipped his tongue inside. Matching his energy, we explored each other. A lick was followed by a twist that morphed into a sucking motion. Tossing my arms over his shoulder, I burrowed my way into the space that still separated us. His caress sent goose pimples up my flesh.

I'd pictured myself kissing this man on several occasions, many of which were during work hours. The fantasies would grind my workday to a halt. I had an active imagination, but my noggin couldn't have dreamt up the fierce yearning we now shared. His beard tickled my nose ever so slightly and I couldn't help but giggle.

"What's so funny?" he asked in between kisses.

"This, you, me ... us."

His sable-colored eyes were weighted and dreamy. Pulling me closer, which I thought was damn near impossible, our lips connected once again. Jamaal's familiar scent was full and robust and now that I was closer than close, the hint of evergreen and citrus had my heart threatening to burst free from my chest.

I couldn't tell you the last time I'd darkened my doorway making kissy faces with a guy. The unexpectedness of it all heightened my desire. His hand was now gently kneading my back as he used the pressure of his palm to shift my chest closer to his. My knees felt like jelly as we swayed back and forth, banging into the doorjamb. Jamaal never unlatched his lips from mine. He was respectful, but I could tell he was greedy for more. Since I was finally able to touch his muscles, I took full advantage, fondling his arms till I had my fill. Which would never happen. I'd never get tired of the sensation of his skin against mine. Jamaal's hand that wasn't inches away from my ass, traveled to the back of my neck. He wrapped his fingers around my neck, drawing out a soft growl from my throat.

When we separated for air, his mouth was painted pink. "I'm glad you came back for the drive by kiss." I wiped at his lips.

"You're a great kisser."

"I've had years of practice. First my teddy bears, then my pillow. Eventually I graduated to skin on skin and started kissing my hand. My first official kiss was with Luke Fuller in an empty tent that smelled like horseshit."

"My first kiss was with a girl named Emily when I was eight. She came up to me and said she liked me before planting a quick peck. Then she punched me in the stomach, and I upchucked all over my shoes. It was right after lunch."

We stared at one another, eventually dissolving into a fit of laughter.

"I don't know why I shared that." Jamaal coughed out while wiping away tears from our giggle fest.

I did. It was because he was officially under my spell. Few men fell, but when they did, it was hard. He may not know it yet, but he and I were going to be sending silly text messages, sharing food off the same plate, and using the same toothbrush before long. Okay maybe not the toothbrush thing because that was kind of gross, but what I was trying to say was that Jamaal Singleton and I went together real bad.

6

On Friday afternoon after work, the company hosted a team building event. Most Fridays there was something fun planned for the staff. It often included music, food, and games. A few weeks ago, Usher performed a mini concert so you know that wasn't cheap. Staff weren't required to attend but there was free food, booze, and entertainment, most people weren't passing up free. Plus, tonight Miles was slated to speak. It would be brief, but he was our leader and no one wanted to miss out on potentially profitable or life affirming information.

Risha and I were walking around checking out the food trucks, deciding on what to eat. We'd already used one of our three free alcohol tickets. I'd gotten an IPA and Risha ordered wine because she was a wino. The event was spread out on the north lawn. It was a spacious entertaining space in the back of the main building with a pond and massive trees providing shade.

"Oh, there he is, our fearless leader. I wonder if he'll mention the expansion," Risha said.

"What do you know about that?"

"People talk. There are several business-related podcasts making predictions online."

Miles walked out of the back entrance of the building followed by his mini entourage, Winnie among them with a notebook in hand and her long braids piled into a bun atop her head. The sight of her took me back to the weight of her juicy, pillowy soft lips pressing against mine. It was all I could think about … I'd kissed the woman of my dreams. On the lips with tongue and it wasn't part of some daydream haze. Was I the luckiest guy in the world? Now statistically this was difficult math, but I felt fairly confident that my life was going better than 99 percent of the men on this orbiting planet.

Risha and I moved closer to the stage to get a better view. The CEO walked past me, making his way to the stage to thunderous applause. Sometimes working at Codeability reminded me of accounts I'd heard of people in a cult. Many of the staff present adored Miles. And they would be willing to do questionable acts if it meant getting in Miles' good graces. The admiration was mostly because he was exactly where they wanted to be. He was thirty-four, the CEO of a Fortune 500 company, and was pictured with the hottest women and most influential celebrities.

I understood the draw. Start-up tech companies like this one usually employed young individuals fresh out of college looking for their piece of the American dream. Half of them thought they could be the next Bill Gates. The other half knew this would look great on their resume in five years and were intrigued by the possibility of stock options.

"Testing one two, one two." The mic gave off a horrible screech. Risha cringed, covering her ears. The next time Miles tried to speak you couldn't hear anything at all but the feedback.

I didn't see help coming, so I headed to the makeshift audio stand right next to the stage and messed with a few cords and buttons. "Try it now," I said, signaling toward Miles.

"Are we good?" This time when he spoke all you could hear was his deep voice loud and crisp. "Thank you, Jamaal. I love that can-do attitude. Jamaal saw a problem and stepped up to fix it. He didn't care that it wasn't his job and he didn't wait for someone else to take charge. Jamaal is a team player. Which we should all strive to be no matter our position in the company.

"When I started Codeability we had a small suite with a leaky roof and spotty Wi-Fi. Can you imagine that? Back then we were the definition of all hands on deck. Do you remember that, Susan?" He pointed to a woman in the crowd who'd been with the company since its inception. "Nice to see that not everything has changed. I don't know Jamaal, I think it may be time for a promotion."

Only when Miles shifted to his prepared remarks did the heat that was flushing my face subside. I hated being the center of attention, and Miles Graves knew that. Taking a long swig of my beer, I tapped Risha on the arm and signaled it was time to search for a less populated spot.

An hour after Miles' speech, Risha and I played a game of Connect Four while trading engineering horror stories with some of our peers.

"What's wrong with your neck?" Risha asked.

"Nothing."

"Then why has it been on a constant swivel for the last hour?"

"I don't know what you're talking about." I stepped forward to drop a red tile into the oversized Connect Four board.

Stepping back, Risha whispered in my ear. "You're looking for Winnie."

"Don't be ridiculous."

"Don't *you* be ridiculous. You like her. Clearly, she likes you because she kissed you."

Yes, I told Risha about movie night with Winnie. She was my best friend and she was a woman and I needed a woman's perspective to make sure I was reading the signs correctly. Winnie kissed me back liked she'd been waiting for a chance to fondle me. Which caught me off guard. I thought I was shooting from mid court with that one. And she initiated, I loved when a woman wasn't afraid to take charge. It was sexy as fuck, took the pressure off me, and boosted my ego like a motherfucker.

"Let's go find her. I can be your wingperson."

"I'm good, thanks." I pushed her forward because it was her turn.

After dropping a tile that won us the game, she returned all smiles. "Listen if I was her and the guy I'd invited to my home and made out with a few nights before didn't so much as bother to say hello, I'd be blocking his number right about now."

I felt a chill coast up my back. "Okay, let's go find her."

So with Risha leading the expedition, I did what any grown man would do, I walked around aimlessly hoping to catch a glimpse of the most beautiful woman here. I found her at a food truck looking much more relaxed than she did earlier accompanying Miles and his crew.

"Are you in line?" I asked, standing behind Winnie. Risha threw me a look that told me I was pathetic.

Winnie spun on her heels, her enigmatic smile overtaking her face. "No, I'm still trying to decide."

"Yep, that's cool."

Risha nudged me, clearing her throat.

"Umm, Winnie, this is my friend, coworker Risha."

Winnie extended her hand. "Nice to meet you. I think I've seen you around the food court once or twice. I remember you were wearing these amazing red shoes. I was tempted to ask you where you got them from."

"The one with the bows?"

"Yeah."

"Aren't they just adorbs. I got them from an online boutique." Risha touched her company badge to the one around Winnie's neck. "I'll message the name. "I must say it's nice to finally meet you. He talks about you all the time."

"Does he?" Winnie flashed me a curious eye.

"Yes, Winnie this and Winnie that. Winnie is beautiful but she is very bad with technology."

I croaked out a nervous chuckle. "Okay, I can already tell this was a mistake."

"No, I like her," Winnie said.

"Ahh, I like you too. Maybe we should all double date." Risha looked at me expectantly. "Don't fuck this up so we can have date nights and Sunday brunches together."

"Worst wingperson ever." I shook my head in disbelief. Risha was supposed to make me look smart and cool, not like a stalker.

"What? She's still here." Risha gestured in Winnie's direction. "Which reminds me I'm not supposed to be. Gotta run because I'm not a single loser."

"Really?" I groaned, tossing my hands in the air at the verbal drive by.

Risha reached for Winnie's arm. "That was intended for him, not you. You are a goddess."

"Bye Risha," I said much louder than I needed to.

"It was so nice to meet you," Winnie gushed.

"Lovely meeting you as well. Have a good night." Before disappearing, Risha stood out of Winnie's line of sight and thrusted her hips back and forth.

"Risha likes embarrassing me."

"She's good at it."

"Yeah, she knows me well."

"How long have you two been friends?"

"Four years. Risha is super dependable and she's a talented software engineer."

"Sounds like she could be a hell of a mentor seeing how you're looking to develop software."

"Yeah, I actually never thought of that." I didn't think of it because Risha and I were already on the same team and I was her boss. I pointed in the direction of the food truck, looking for a distraction. "It's hard to go wrong with a corn dog."

"I think this is my favorite by far." There wasn't a line and Winnie placed her order for a Cheeto corn dog and a strawberry daiquiri from the neighboring adult beverage cart, handing over tickets to both vendors. "Do you want anything?

"Nope. I'm good."

When her food arrived, we found a tall table where she could eat.

"Are you on a break?"

"No, actually I'm done for the night. Now that the boss is away I get to have a little bit of fun."

"Speaking of which, this turned out great. You should be super proud."

"All I did was book food trucks, entertainment, and arrange the vendor placement."

"Yeah, and without that we'd be standing on an empty lawn."

"I guess you're right." She hopped a shoulder.

"Damn right I am. You're amazing. Own that shit."

Winnie took a massive bite out of her Cheeto crusted corn dog. Cheeto dust settled on the side of her mouth.

"You have a little ..." I pointed to her lips with a wiggle of my finger.

"I do?" Winnie asked, around a mouth full of food. She licked at the right side of her mouth, totally missing the orange hued crumbs on her left side.

"Let me." I extended my hand, brushing the side of her lip with the pad of my thumb. Bringing my hand to my mouth, I licked the salty snack dust from my thumb. "All better."

Winnie eyed me in silence for a moment before asking, "Do you want to—"

"Yes. Whatever it is. Yes." It didn't matter what the ask was, as long as we got to spend time together, I was down for anything.

Winnie gathered her corn dog and drink and led the way. We walked for a while, talking about work and office gossip. She knew everything. During the course of our short walk, I was up to speed on who was getting a divorce, who was seeing each other after hours, and who was about to get fired. Winnie stopped at an adult sized inflatable jump house which had long lines earlier in the night when Risha and I were walking around. But right now it was a bit of a ghost town.

"I've been thinking about this place since I booked it months ago."

"Let's do it," I said, pulling back the flap so she could walk inside.

When we entered the tent, it was a mind fuck because the space was not at all what I expected. The bounce house was triple the size of ones you'd find at a kid's party. In the center of the room was a massive trampoline and the remaining space that wasn't jumpable housed tables and chairs. It was apparent from the forgotten plastic cups and partially finished plates of food that this spot had seen a ton of action tonight.

"You rented a trampoline?"

"Yeah, you know Miles Graves's motto. Go big or go home."

"I've never heard him say that."

"Well, you're not an executive. Not yet anyway."

"What's that supposed to mean?"

"You heard Miles tonight. He was very impressed by you," she half teased.

"I just fixed the mic. Anyone could have done that shit."

"But it wasn't anyone, it was you. And Miles seemed to appreciate it." She absentmindedly started to clear away plates, chucking them into a nearby trash can.

"I thought you were off the clock?"

"I am."

I reached for her hand and made a mental note about the symmetrical proportions of her hand in relation to mine. It was a perfect fit. "Then stop working."

"Sorry, habit."

"No, I get it. You do know that's the goal with this company. For the staff to always be working but not realize it because of the amenities. Everything is right here on campus so you never have to leave, it's more than just convenience, it's created this way by design. Because they know employees will put in more hours and rarely access the extra perks during work days. And since everyone is a salary worker, it's essentially free labor after five o'clock."

"I read an article recently that more start-up employees are suffering from burnout and anxiety."

"I believe it because I stay stressed."

"You do?" Winnie's face took on a look of concern.

"Yeah, big time."

"But you make everything look so easy. Like you have it all figured out." Winnie was really big on eye contact and her intense eyes were locked on me. Even though it felt like her shrewd gaze was assessing all my insecurities and regrets, I didn't shy away from it. Because part of me believed that being cared for by this woman came with healing properties.

"I can assure you I do not know what the fuck I'm doing, or what I want to do, or where I want to be. My family doesn't help any either."

"I get it. Family seemed to specialize in a unique form of peer pressure. I had to let my mom know I wasn't her mini me and she couldn't weigh me down with her unfulfilled dreams."

"I think parents just put a lot of expectations on their kids. Not fully realizing how that affects them."

"So what does your family want you to do?" Winnie asked.

"Be ambitious."

"And you don't want that?" She fidgeted with one of the rings on her finger.

"I want to be content." I shrugged. "It's not about the things. It's never about the things. It's about the people, the friendships, the bonds we build. Don't get me wrong, I'm not saying I want to struggle. I just don't want to chase the newest and the bestest thing. Does that make sense?"

"I get it. When is enough enough?"

"For my family it's never enough."

"My dad always says. 'If you want to be happy, be true to yourself.' When my mom ran away with my dad all he had was a rundown RV and a scrappy demeanor. And they've been sickeningly in love ever since." She narrowed her eyes. "Which may be why I suck at relationships. I compare everything to what my parents have and most people aren't looking to go that deep romantically."

"What do you mean?"

"I mean ... I don't know if I can put it into words, it's more of a feeling. Love lives in the unspoken moments."

My eyes darted across her face. Like Winnie, I couldn't articulate love but I knew what it felt like and would definitely be able to recognize it if I ever felt it again. Being in love, truly being in love was beyond simple words. It was a heartbeat normally unnoticed but ever present.

"All I know is your dad must have had a whole lotta swag to pull your mother with a dollar and a dream."

"I guess he did. I'll have to show you pictures of them sometime. They were pretty hot."

"They would have to be because ..." I waved my hand in her direction.

"Shut up, I'm not hot." She snorted a laugh as if trying to prove her point.

I stood directly in front of her. "You should know something about me. When I give someone a compliment, I hate it when they try to negate my words."

"I'm sorry."

I'm sorry too. Sorry we had all these fucking clothes on.

"Don't be sorry just accept that when it comes to the hotness meter, you're off the Richter."

"Thank you, but ... thank you."

"So did you bring me here to talk or are you trying to get active?"

"Umm ..."

"From jumping on the trampoline."

"Yes, let's do it."

Before climbing up, we removed our shoes. I wobbled for a bit trying to get my footing but Winnie was a natural, leaping like a professional. In an attempt to match her energy, I jumped higher than my comfort zone, and upon landing, I felt the vibrations in my teeth. Of course, I played it cool, nothing to see here. Just a grown ass man being humbled by a person who required a step stool to reach the top shelf. *That wasn't a fair jab because truthfully, occasionally I had to bust out a stool, but you get my point.*

For someone so small, she had a ton of power and was far more limber than me. She bounced off the trampoline and performed a split midair. Her next trick involved backflips that spanned the length of the springy surface. What made this all the more impressive was the fact that she was wearing a fuzzy, checkered cardigan and wide-legged jeans. I tried my best to keep my thoughts PG-13, but all I could think about was her contorting into a Bavarian pretzel while she rode my dick.

"So is this the type of stuff your family does?" I asked, settling into a slow bounce.

"Yes, I come from a long line of tumblers."

"Chambers and sons, right?"

"Yes, when my dad branched out on his own, he changed the name to the Catapulting Chambers."

"Did you bring me here to embarrass me?" I teased. "Because truthfully the two beers I drank are sloshing around in my stomach."

"No, I would never." A sly smile took over her face. "Maybe I brought you here to see how nimble you are."

"I'm not known for being spry, but I make up for it in other ways." I licked at my bottom lip. *My tongue was nimble and I was ready to prove it.*

The thing about people like me and Winnie was we were raised to follow these arbitrary rules of engagement. Flirting became a balancing act. I didn't want to come off as some womanizer and she didn't want to be perceived as a slut. So I played the role of the respectable stand-up guy. Don't get me wrong, I was all those things, but I also had visions of pulling her hair and fucking her face.

I dropped to the mat to give my stomach a chance to settle.

Winnie walked toward me with such grace despite the shaky surface. When she was close enough, she dropped to her knees, crawling the rest of the way until she was directly in front of me. Her perfectly coiffed bun had slid free and her braids were framing her face.

"God you're pretty."

"Hot and pretty. You're great for my ego."

"I may wear glasses, but my eyes still work. And you are beautiful." I tucked a few of her braids behind her ear before resting my hand on her neck. Gently, I guided her forward until her face was inches from mine. The sweet floral scent of gardenia and another flower tickled my nostrils. I only recognized the gardenia because my parents had some planted in their backyard. That scent was just another reason why Winnie felt so familiar to me.

The sultry whisper of her breath as she exhaled initiated a shiver that licked up my spine. When she smiled at me, there were countless words behind her mink-brown eyes. Winnie's hand dropped to my thigh and the muscle underneath twitched at her touch. My arm encircled her waist as I pulled her onto my lap to straddle me. She pressed her hand to my chest and I was certain she could hear the mess her touch made of my heart.

My gaze lingered on her modest breast which rose and fell. When I leaned closer, her lips parted, inviting me in for a kiss. I captured her plump lips between mine, our tongues twirling and licking the others. She tasted sweet, probably from the daiquiri she'd been drinking on the way over here. Winnie wrapped her arms around me and the sensation of her toned, yet soft body flipped a switch in my brain. I moaned against her mouth and her hips started to float over my lap, causing my dick to stiffen underneath her.

Unlocking our lips, I ventured to lay my mouth on other parts of her body. Whipping her hair over her shoulder, I nuzzled my face into her neck. Licking my way upward until I reached her ear.

"You are a fucking ten," I said, stating the obvious. My mouth latched on to her earlobe and gave a suck. Winnie emitted sounds that drove me wild. The uptick in her breath. The random one-word statements. "Wow" and "Yes" letting me know I was on the right path. When we finally kissed again, my back floated to the mat and I could feel the weight of her body. Winnie continued to work her crotch into mine. Grabbing hold of her ass, I helped her roll her hips, wanting her to feel every inch of me hard and ready for her.

"You feel so good," she whispered.

Being this close was torture and ecstasy in the same moment. I never wanted a woman more than I wanted the quirky, sexy vision that was Winnie. But despite the sexual desire swirling inside me, my rational side kicked in and started screaming in my ear about sex in public places and questioning if this trampoline had ever been sanitized. Just imagining how many stinky feet jumped on the trampoline was turning my stomach.

Can you get athletes' feet on your penis?

Pressing back on Winnie's waist, I sat up. This was probably the first time either of us had come up for air in the past several minutes.

"Why'd you stop?" she asked breathlessly.

"Because if we don't stop I will fuck you on this trampoline."

"I mean. I would really like that for me," she timidly offered.

I swallowed hard. The woman of my dreams was literally circling her hips over my crotch and looking down at me with "Fuck me" eyes and I was ruining the moment. Call me a prude, but I didn't want our first time to be on a sketchy trampoline in a tent that smelled like booze. Plus, we weren't actually in a secluded location. Anyone could walk in on us. I'd never gotten caught with my dick out at work and I wasn't going to start today.

I get sex in public places can be exciting, but it forces you to rush, and how can you fully commit to the moment if you're always listening for approaching footsteps? The last thing I wanted to do was rush my sexual experience with Winnie. I wanted to languish in it. I wanted to stop for snacks and witty banter in between. I did not want to pump and dump.

Shifting my body, I gently pushed her off my lap. The front of my jeans was distorted from the enlarged dick bulging against the denim. Winnie's jaw hung slack and her lipstick was smeared across her mouth, so I know that meant my face looked like Ronald McDonald. I averted my eyes and immediately started to picture images of puppies and kittens frolicking in a field. Anything to stop the thought of Winnie attempting to fit my dick in her mouth.

"Did I do something wrong?"

"Nope. We're at work. And this is a trampoline."

"We can go somewhere else. Your place, my place, a parked car."

I wanted to have sex with Winnie. But I didn't want our first time to be tonight. Our first time should be special. I wasn't spontaneous, I was a planner. And I always thought we'd have sex after a great date, with engaging conversation and flirting that became increasingly more provocative throughout the night. On the ride home from said date, we'd be on pins and needles because at this point it was painful trying to resist our obvious attraction. When we got back to my place, we'd tumble into the living room already kissing and shedding clothes. And we'd both laugh because we were nervous and excited.

"I should go," Winnie said.

"What?" Winnie was already climbing off the mat. "If you want to have sex now, we can have sex now."

"If I want to?" Her brows mashed together and the expression on her face was one I was acquainted with but had never seen from her before. Anger.

Fuck.

I dismounted the trampoline with all the grace of a baby giraffe just learning to walk. Stepping into my shoes I glanced at her annoyed face. "Are you mad at me?"

"I'm not interested in pressuring you to have sex. And if you're not into me in that way, I understand. Maybe we should just be friends or coworkers."

So less than friends?

"Are you out of your fucking mind?" *How could she not know how into her I was?* There's this theory that if a guy really likes you and you ask him to peel an orange, he will without hesitation. I would peel her orange, run her bathwater, and grab an extra blanket in the middle of the night when she's cold. "Winnie all I do is think—" My words were followed by laughter from a group of people entering the tent behind us.

"I should go."

"I wish you'd stay."

"It's late. I'm tired and Simone's home alone." Before her words fully registered, she was already headed for the exit.

I wanted to scream across the tent "I desperately want to fuck you." But that conversation would have to wait for another time.

7

IT WAS SIX O'CLOCK IN THE MORNING AND I WAS IN MY bed with a package of animal crackers and several empty wine cooler bottles. The entire drive home the night before, I was shell-shocked. Thank God muscle memory kicked in because I don't remember pulling into my parking spot. I was too preoccupied with replaying the events of the last hour to pinpoint the exact moment I'd fucked up. Everything was going so well and in an instant, Jamaal was pushing me away and being cavalier. My lack of sleep did not provide me with any answers.

Did I suck at reading people? Mhm ... maybe a little bit. When I was nine, I thought Marcia Gross and I were BFF's for life, only to find out she hated my guts and thought I smelled like curry. My mother was from the Caribbean, of course we smelled like curry. But I thought my instincts were spot on about Jamaal. He invited himself to my house to watch a movie. He kissed me good night ... no, shit that was me. But he kissed me back. Or maybe he was just being polite. But his dick was hard, you can't fake that.

He asked me on a date for Saturday, which was today and was now clearly cancelled because I came on way too strong. Simone said men liked women who took charge. What's more boss than initiating sex and giving a man the green light to put you through the headboard? Maybe Jamaal didn't like aggressive women. Perhaps he preferred his women mild and I was extra spicy.

He introduced me to his friend, Risha. Why would he do that if he wasn't interested? Because he was interested until he wasn't. It all went to shit in the tent when I dry humped his lap and reached for his dick. I went from hot to wackadoo real quick.

There was a knock at my bedroom door.

"Come in," I grunted, my voice was deep and throaty, still clouded with the little sleep I managed to get.

"You're still in bed?"

"Yeah, where else would I be? I'm sad but not jump off a bridge sad."

"We're supposed to go to the fun run." Simone offered up an apologetic smile.

"Is that today?"

"Yes."

No. Absolutely the fuck not. I was going to stay in this bed all day with the exception of bathroom and food breaks. My laptop would be streaming *Girlfriends* so I could feel slightly better about my life, because Joan's was so messed up.

Simone pulled the covers from my bed. "The run will get your mind off of Jamaal—"

"Don't say his name."

"I'm not going to let you mope in bed all weekend over that asshole."

I cringed at her words. He wasn't an asshole. He was amazing, and smart, and his dick was big and I'd ruined all that.

Simone chanted, "Fun run, fun run, fun run."

"You know that's an oxymoron right? Fun and running do not go together."

"Get up, Chambers. We leave in thirty minutes."

There was no use in protesting. I'd agreed to this months ago. Begrudgingly, I hopped in the shower before throwing on some shorts, a supportive sports bra and a loose-fitting T-shirt. I gathered my braids and secured them in a high ponytail. On the way out the door, Simone tossed me a granola bar and handed me a smoothie and we were off.

In the high seventies, the weather was perfect for a run. My mood on the other hand was not. I'd come on entirely too strong and now Jamaal was probably weirded out and would never want to talk to me again. I couldn't even blame my actions on the alcohol because I was stone cold sober. The past few months, physical contact with someone from the opposite sex had been sparse.

Raymonte the barista at the café at work would often personally hand me my drink orders. Each time brushing his hand against mine. That was the extent of my skin-on-skin action, I was wandering through the desert squinting in search of a puddle of water. I needed to be fucked stat. Jamaal must think I'm some kind of freaky provocateur who gets off on the thrill of exhibition sex. For the record the weirdest place I'd engaged in sex was a van. A windowless van, so I was far from having a voyeurism kink.

After signing in and receiving our numbers, we lined up. Simone was a professional, she ran all the time. I was a novice and the thought of running when no one was chasing me was disconcerting. But shortly after we moved in together, I told her running in a marathon was something I'd always wanted to do. That was a lie, but we were new roommates and I wanted it to work, so I may have feigned my interest a bit.

Simone agreed to run at my pace for the first fifteen minutes, but after she was going to meet me at the finish line. As we lined up alongside the other running fanatics, I scanning the crowd, looking for someone I could beat. Sure it's not about finishing first but I didn't want to finish dead last. I spied an older woman with sweat bands on her head and wrist. I could out run a senior citizen ... right?

What would possess hundreds of people to get up early on a Saturday, which was made for sleeping in and going to brunch, to lace up their sneakers and run in mass? It was sick, disgusting even. I should be rolling over in bed right now, not teeing up to roll an ankle. Which was the best possible outcome. Knowing my luck, I'd end up being carted away in an ambulance. Was it too late to claim my asthma was acting up? My inhaler was in my fanny pack and I'd been semi training these past few weeks in preparation but ...

I continued to scope out my fellow runners. So many of them appeared amped to be here. I'd heard of the runners high but I thought that came after the run. There was a father here with who I assumed was his daughter, she couldn't have been more than ten years old. When I was ten my parents at least let us watch cartoons and eat one bowl of sugary cereal before we had to practice our routine for that night's show. Now as an adult my weekends were sacred and after today would never be sullied with activities requiring physical exertion. Hiking ... out. Long walks on a sandy beach ... out. Hills ... hell to the nah.

Next to me was a redhead with hot pink shoes. On the opposite side, Simone was stretching, and just a few feet in front of me was a very familiar frame. A man in running shorts that showed off his muscular thighs was shaking out his legs. This fucker broke my heart and thought he'd go for a leisurely run?

"Jamaal?" My tone was a bit more aggressive than I intended.

He spun around just as surprised to see me as I was him. "Winnie, what are you doing here?"

"Running." I tugged at the number 481 pinned to my shirt.

Simone grabbed my arm and pulled me away. No excuse me. No nice to see you again, Jamaal just a swift jerk. She positioned us on the opposite side of the running path. "He doesn't get to make you cry and then act like the good guy."

"Technically, he didn't *make* me cry."

"He led you on and then couldn't handle that you were sexually liberated."

"Is that what I am?"

We didn't have a chance to say much else, the horn blared and everyone was off. For the first few minutes, Jamaal maintained a steady pace a few feet ahead of us. But eventually I lost him in the throng of participants. I promised Simone I would run as fast as I could for the first half so she didn't fall too far behind her target pace. When we reached the fifteen minute mark Simone gave me a big smile and said, "Meet you at the finish line." before sprinting away.

Now that I was alone, I could slow down a bit. I scanned the area looking for the older woman from the starting line, but she was nowhere to be found. Jamaal was also nowhere in sight. The further I ran, the more irritated I became. "Stupid marathon. Stupid Simone." I grumbled under my breath. And what was Jamaal doing here? He'd mentioned running but I was thinking treadmill, not outdoor. But it made perfect sense he was lean and toned. My head craned as I tried to catch a glimpse of him with his legs out. All I saw were a group of focused runners. Jamaal was probably damn near at the finish line by now.

God his shorts practically clung to him, giving me ass, thighs and calves. I bet he was all sweaty and every muscle in his body was on swole. Shaking the vision from my brain, I did my best to concentrate on the road ahead. It was 8:25 in the morning, far too early to cream my shorts over Jamaal. Which was just another reason he was probably scared off. My aura was giving desperate. When I reached the hill, all the gas in my tank was depleted. I was having a difficult time making it to the top, when a strong hand rested on the small of my back.

"You got this," Jamaal said.

"No I do not," I replied, completely out of breath.

"This is the hard part. When you think you can't and you want to give up. You need to push through it." His hand never left my back as he kept pace with my unsure steps.

"I think I'm going to piss my pants."

"Don't do that. But you do have permission to cry, yell, or cuss. Just don't give up on yourself."

Nodding, I wiped sweat from my eyes. When we made it to the top of the hill, I felt it, my second wind kicking in. I don't know where it came from but my legs seemed stronger and my breathing was less erratic. Maybe it was because I'd just conquered that mammoth hill, but I was invigorated. Jamaal's hand dropped from my back and he slowly picked up the pace and my limbs moved in unison with his.

"That's it just like that. Good girl," he encouraged me.

My already flushed face grew hotter. *I was a good girl.* For the last few minutes, I went stride for stride with Jamaal, never letting him get too far ahead. It was clear he wasn't looking to ditch me because while his words of affirmation had kicked me into overdrive, I was sure he could smoke me if he really wanted to.

Jamaal's watch chimed and he turned to me. "Just a little bit further. You got this Winn-Dixie. Don't make me finish alone."

First, he called me Winn-Dixie. I think my heart melted in my chest. My dad used to call me Winn-Dixie when I was a kid. Second, I was actually going to complete this damn fun run because of him.

With the finish line in sight, Jamaal winked at me and we made our final push. Crossing the line, a sense of accomplishment washed over me. I did a hard thing and succeeded. This was my Mount Everest. I'd braved the balmy mid-seventies weather and treacherous terrain of sloped hills and narrow curves and come out on top. Throwing my arms around a sweaty Jamaal, I squeezed him tight.

"I would not have finished without you. I was about to quit and text Simone to meet me at the waffle house."

Jamaal clutched my waist. "That was all you."

Pulling away, I was greeted by a sincere smile. How could I ever be mad at this man? "My hands are shaking."

"That's normal. You're just coming down from pure adrenaline. It'll wear off." Jamaal lifted his shirt to wipe his face, revealing his toned chest. I averted my eyes, not wanting to stare. "Should we go and get our medals?"

"Sure." Pulling a granola bar out of my pack, I ripped it in two, offering him half.

"Thanks." He popped the bite into his mouth.

If I hoped to salvage any type of friendship, I needed to address the elephant trotting along next to us.

"Listen, I'm sorry about last night. I made you uncomfortable and I own that. It was never my intention. I was just excited. Hanging out with you, being close to you was nice, and I didn't want it to end. If you're not interested I totally get it. I just hope we can still be friends."

"Winnie, the last thing I want is to be your friend."

"But last night—"

"Last night was bad timing. On our date tonight I promise I'll be in sync."

"I wasn't sure that was still happening."

"Of course it is. Unless ... unless you don't want it too?"

"Oh my God, there you are." Simone approached us with a frazzled expression. "I was going to start calling the hospitals."

"I'm fine."

"I called you like a dozen times."

I pulled out my phone and scrolled through the several missed call notifications. "My bad."

"Hello again." Simone shot Jamaal a side eye and her tone was cold and dismissive.

I'd told her about how Jamaal left me high and dry. Or maybe I should say horny and wet. My retelling of last night's events was heavy on me being the wronged party. So now Simone hated Jamaal because she thought I still hated him. To be fair at no point did I say I hated him. I did tell her my feelings were hurt and I may have cried a little.

"Nice seeing you again," Jamaal replied.

"Are you ready to go?" Simone was standing in between me and Jamaal in an attempt to ice him out.

I flashed her a pleading look but she wasn't picking up what my exaggerated eyes were putting down. Quickly I sent her a text message that read *Abort Project Jamaal Sucks.*

Simone glanced at the face of her dinging phone and after reading my message, her entire demeanor changed. "Jamaal, it was so nice bumping into you again. Winnie, I'll meet you at the car."

Jamaal's brows mashed together as we watched Simone walk away. "That was kind of weird."

"That's Simone. If I had to describe her in one word it would be weird."

Shifting his focus solely on me, he said, "You didn't answer my question."

I closed the distance between us, hoping to God my deodorant was still working. "The answer is yes. But you already knew that."

"Great, I'll pick you up at six."

Displaying a flirty smile, I walked away. I didn't get five steps before my left leg caught a charley horse and I slid to the grass. "Ouch, ouch."

Jamaal came rushing to my side. "Are you alright?"

"Yeah, it's a charley horse," I said through the pain.

He reached for the leg I was clutching and massaged my tight muscles until the cramp subsided.

"All better?"

"Yeah, much better." He helped me back on to my feet. "Thanks."

"No worries. Make sure you ice it when you get home."

"Will do." This time I limped away in shame, letting go of any attempt at being sexy.

8

FOLLOWING THE RACE, I HEADED TO MY PARENT'S house. The entire drive there, all I could think about was Winnie. I never expected her to be at the marathon. It had to be fate working in my favor because we were in the same place at the same time and despite the large crowd, we found one another.

She looked even prettier in the morning sans makeup, her hair pulled back highlighting her face. She possessed many stunning features, but her face was the showstopper. The cheekbones, the deep-set eyes, the freckles that were more pronounced with a clean face. And then there were her lips, full and pouty with a hint of peachy gloss.

I thought it would take days, maybe weeks to dig myself out of the hole I'd created the night before. Winnie wanted me. Me. And I treated the offer of pussy like a serving of liver and onions. The fact that I caused her to question my intentions even slightly upset me. But we were in a better place now. She knew I was down and tonight, with her permission, I hoped to prove it.

Pulling into my parent's driveway in a gated community in Carmel Valley, I spotted a familiar Porsche parked out front. I didn't visit as often as I should but when I did, the memories came flooding back. This long driveway was where I'd scribble for hours with chalk. And this tree-lined block was the backdrop as I learned to ride a bicycle.

Inside, I found my mother in the family room tinkering on the piano. "Today is just full of surprises," she said, rising from the bench with open arms. She enveloped me in a tight hug. The smell of roses filled my nostril as I kissed the top of her head. Phyllis Singleton was a lady of leisure. At fifty-eight, she spent her days at the posh gym gossiping with her snooty friends. At night, you could find her dressed to the nines in attendance at some charity gala or premiere event. "To what do I owe the pleasure? She pulled back, giving my outfit a critical eye. "And why are you dressed like that?"

"I received an urgent text message from your nephew asking me to meet him here." I ignored the comment about my attire.

I was on my way home after the marathon when my watch started to vibrate. Checking my wrist, a message from my knuckle-head cousin popped up.

"Meet me at your parents' house. I need to pick your brain about something. Importance: High. Do not ignore me or I'll tell Aunt Phyllis it was you who broke that vase when we were nine."

So like I always did, I dropped everything to help my oh so needy kin.

I walked with my mom to the kitchen to grab a drink. "This place looks nice. Have you been redecorating?" This was kind of a stupid question. My mother was always redecorating, claiming she needed to redistribute the positive energy. Whatever that meant.

"Just sprucing the place up for the big Summer Society event I'm hosting next month."

My face was blank.

"You are coming aren't you?"

"Umm—"

"Jamaal, I told you about this months ago. This is really important to me. I want the whole family there."

"If it's important to you then I will be there with bells on." I scanned the butler's pantry looking for something to snack on before settling for some Oreos displayed like an art installation in a glass jar on the kitchen island. Before I could even remove the lid, my mother chastised me.

"No, not those. They're for aesthetics only."

"Cookies are meant to be eaten, not admired."

"You know how when I come to visit you and you never let me touch your Lego collection. This is the same thing." She winked.

"Some of those Lego projects took me days to put together."

"I never thought I'd be talking about plastic building blocks with my grown son."

"I could be in and out of rehab like cousin Pete."

My mother swatted my arm. "That's not funny. You kids these days think everything is a joke."

"He's a sex addict. I mean it's kind of funny."

She opened the jar and handed me four cookies. "The party is Carmel Valley chic so get your linen suit dry cleaned."

Yes, I owned a linen suit, two actually. Like I said, my parents liked to entertain. And in Carmel Valley, California, even a summer brunch came with formalities.

"Yes ma'am," I said between chews. "Where's the boy prince at? I saw his car out front."

"He's upstairs in your old bedroom. Said he was looking for something."

I kissed my mother on the cheek and headed up the stairs two at a time. Entering my childhood bedroom, I made my presence known. "It smells like punk ass bitch in here."

"Negro, that's your upper lip." Miles stuck his head out of my bedroom closet. "Why are your legs out?"

Glancing down at my running shorts, I knew I should've stopped to change before heading over here. Miles and I were constantly snapping on one another, and I'd just given him fuel to add to the insult fire. "Don't worry about it, sweetheart. Why are you snooping through my things?"

"I'm looking for our stash of nudie magazines from when we were little," he joked.

"I gave those to your dad. He said he needed inspiration." I laughed.

"Fuck you."

"So what's up? You texted me 911. Where's the fire?"

"In your tight ass shorts. You should probably get that checked out."

"I like the tingle."

Miles Graves was my cousin. Our mothers were sisters. And since we were a year apart in age, we grew up doing everything together. I didn't have a brother, but Miles was a good replacement. He liked to pretend he came from humble beginnings. But that was a gross exaggeration. Miles and I experienced the soft life growing up. My mom and aunt came from long money, generational wealth, and the top echelons of Black excellence. Both women married equally impressive men, our dads.

So that meant winters in Aspen and summers in the Amalfi Coast. Tennis lessons and piano recitals. My eye still twitched when I heard Beethoven's "Moonlight Sonata." When Miles needed start-up money, my aunt and uncle fronted him the cash with no questions asked. Anything for their prodigal son.

With the exception of Risha, no one at work knew Miles and I were related. Miles didn't care but it was important to me to not be labeled a nepotism hire. I was good at what I did, hella good. When Miles approached me about joining Codeability, he said it was his dream to have a family business and work alongside me as his "brother." Despite my reluctance, Miles was a born salesman. He could convince a genie to buy a new lamp. Since elementary he was hustling kids out of things he didn't even need just because he could.

I remembered our conversation like it was yesterday.

"Listen I appreciate the offer, Miles, I really do but I don't think it's a good fit," I said.

"So what are you going to do? They are wasting your talents at BioMed and from the rumors your CEO is about to be breaking big rocks into smaller rocks in prison."

"I don't think they make people do that anymore."

"Whatever. You should've been with Codeability from its inception but you're so fucking stubborn."

"I just don't want shit handed to me. I'm not afraid of a little hard work."

"Neither am I, but what is the point of being born into privilege if you don't use it every now and then. Shit the Chads and Jetts of the world sure the hell are so why not us. That's the problem with Black folks, we always feel like we have to struggle out the mud."

"What mud are you talking about? The mud bath at the country club."

"BioMed isn't going to make it another quarter. Your misplaced loyalty is going to have you unemployed. And you can't stay with me when you get kicked out of your tacky one-bedroom apartment."

"First off, my apartment isn't tacky. Second, I just want to earn my place. I've never been one looking for handouts."

"Bitch that ain't a handout. They should've never allowed your, 'please sir may I have some more' looking ass to be born into money." Miles huffed out a long breath.

He was right, we were built differently. Miles relished the lavish life. Expensive cars, perpetual vacations, and endless parties. Me on the other hand, I just wanted to live a modest life with a woman who made me feel like the luckiest man alive. I wasn't looking to flex. Yes, we were wealthy. Yes, I received a substantial trust fund when I turned twenty-five, but I wasn't about the rich party boy life.

Miles walked over to me leaning his forehead into mine. "Shit Jamaal, I need you. You are the smartest engineer I know. I don't trust anybody like I trust you. What did we say when we were coming up?"

"Brothers for life."

"I need my brother by my side."

So I acquiesced and the rest is history.

"What do you want that it couldn't wait until Monday?" I asked, plopping down on the queen-sized bed.

"I had an idea for a new logo. For the expansion. I'm interested in those doodles you used to create?"

"My drawings. What about them?"

"Do you remember that design you would tag everything with? Your binder, your locker at school, any writable surface really. You were obsessed with that design for like two whole summers. It had a circle and triangle with some squiggly lines or some shit."

"You made me come to my momma's house on a Saturday over some random drawing?"

"Random back then. The face of our newest project now."

"You are fucking unbelievable." Miles was a taker always had been. Frankly, I was surprised he was asking. He was more of a do whatever he wanted and then offer a fake apology later type of guy. "The world doesn't revolve around you."

"I checked with my mom and she disagrees." He offered a smug smirk.

"Well of course not. As far as Aunt Marsha is concerned, her Milesy Wilesy can't do any wrong."

"Doesn't suck being the golden child."

"You said spoiled entitled brat wrong." I stood, opening a random notebook to a blank page. With pencil in hand, I tried to recreate the image Miles was referring to. Ripping the sheet from the book, I handed it to him.

"This is it." He chuckled, turning the paper over in his hands. "This is the logo for Synergy."

"Synergy?"

"Expansion is amongst us my friend. Speaking of which, are you done slumming? Are you ready to join the big boys?"

"Miles, we talked about this. I'm happy where I'm at."

"When I asked you to come work at Codeability I meant

beside me not in the basement. I respect you want to work your way up and all that but this is ridiculous. You're an engineer and you're over here trouble shooting audio issues. Good looking out by the way." He tagged my shoulder.

"And then you used the moment to embarrass the shit out of me. Thanks for that."

"I was just having some fun. I wasn't the only one. I spotted you laughing and chatting it up with my assistant, Winifred."

I told you Miles knew her name. He had a photographic memory or something because he remembered everyone.

"You mean Winnie. Yeah, what about it?"

"She's hot in a librarian kind of way."

I wagged my finger at him. "Absolutely not. She's off limits. Winnie is a good girl."

I had to make it very clear I was claiming dibs. Miles had always been the center of attention. We were both nerds growing up, but he was the tall handsome nerd and I was the nerd who sported glasses, braces, and had a bad case of acne. Needless to say the ladies were never checking for me when Miles was in the room. It took me several years, a good dentist, a strict skin care routine, and a significant growth spurt in college before I felt confident in my body.

"If she's a good girl then why is she hanging out with you?"

I faked a laugh. "Very funny. I'm serious. Winnie is off limits. I'm actively pursuing that."

"Chill out. When have I ever stolen your girl?"

"Payton Zimmer, ninth grade."

"Payton Zimmer was not checking for you and your dumb knock-knock jokes. Payton Zimmer wanted to be felt up in a vacant classroom."

"I was working up to that," I huffed.

"We do not have the same taste in women. I like super models and you like school teachers."

"Shit, school teachers are hot. You remember Ms. Truman?"

"Do I. I think I got a sprained wrist because of that woman."
My features turned sour. "You always take it too far."
"What?" He hopped an innocent shoulder.

9

WE WERE ON THE I-5 DESTINATION UNKNOWN. JAMAAL only suggested I should dress comfortably with the admonition against wearing heels. I'd opted for a gingham A-line dress that stopped well above my knees and a pair of white Converse sneakers. I knew I'd chosen correctly when I opened my apartment door and Jamaal's mouth dropped.

After a thirty-minute drive which ended up at the San Diego Bay, Jamaal parked the car and rounded the vehicle, opening my door. When I stepped out he pointed in the direction of the water. "Your chariot awaits."

Squinting my eyes, I asked, "What am I supposed to be looking at?"

Claiming my hand, we walked closer. "It's a cocktail cruise," he said with excitement.

"Cocktail cruise?"

"Yep, alcohol, food, and the sunset."

I pulled my face, making an impressed expression. "Okay I'm down."

Even though I'd lived in California, I'd hardly visited the beach or the bay. When I first moved here, I remember coming to the beach and taking pictures. I texted them to my family with the message "Wish you were here." My brother wrote back with a "Beware of Jaws." I'm sure my parents and siblings thought my days were spent frolicking on the beach, not schlepping coffee to my demanding boss.

As part of a traveling circus, we'd been to California plenty of times. But we were never in one place long enough to enjoy the sights. A visit to the bay and a sunset cruise was a bucket list item, that now thanks to Jamaal, I could tick off. We followed a laughing couple and climbed aboard. The ship was called the California Spirit with indoor and outdoor seating. This was a popular attraction because the vessel was practically at capacity. We'd managed to snag a discreet table in the corner which allowed for great views of the city and the ability to people watch. In short order, we were sailing away, and the bar was opened for business.

Jamaal returned from the bar with two drinks. Something fruity for me and a beer for him along with a menu. After perusing the items, we ordered several small bites and I was now attempting to learn more about him.

"Tell me about your family? I feel like I know nothing about them."

"Not really much to tell. Mom and Dad are still together. I have a younger sister who at twenty-eight is still a pain in my ass."

"Small family?

"It's just the four of us but my extended family is huge and we're all pretty close."

"So you're big on backyard barbecues and family reunions with matching T-shirts?"

"Backyard barbecues not so much. A summer soiree? Definitely." He paused, taking a swig of his beer. "Don't think you're going to pepper me with questions all night. I got some for you too."

"Shoot."

"What was your role in the traveling circus?"

"Really, that's what you want to know?"

"You don't casually mention you grew up in a circus and not expect follow-up inquiries."

"Fair enough. Well you had the Catapulting Chambers and

then my brothers and sister and I were in an aerobatic dance trope."

"Like Cirque du Soleil?"

"Cirque du Soleil but with hip-hop and African infused beats."

"How long did you do that?"

"Since I could walk. I'd perform flips and choreographed dances. Think when a parent would have Junior show off his dance moves to their friends. It was like that but on a bigger scale. As I got older the flips got more elaborate and death defying. We'd do syncopated tumbling and my brothers would toss me in the air and catch me. Or balance me with one hand."

"That's hella impressive. Do you miss it?"

"I miss the people more than anything. Before I went away to college it was all I'd known. But the constant travel, never being able to make new friends was exhausting. We were homeschooled so I didn't get to be a cheerleader or sign up for the archery club. There were no proms or homecomings. I never got to sneak off with the popular jock after school. Granted I probably wouldn't have been dating the jock or been a part of the popular clique, but in my fifteen-year-old daydreams I was."

"In real life high school wasn't like any of that shit they aired on the Disney channel."

"What are you saying, you weren't popular?"

"Look at me. I'm five eleven and I wear glasses. I was never the popular kid. I sucked at sports. I was part of the school newspaper and in the AV and robotics club."

"So you've always been smart?"

"Smart, yes. Did I have a burgeoning social life and dates? No."

"If I'd attended your high school I would've dated you."

"Ahh, thanks."

"No seriously. You're intelligent, funny, and good looking."

"I didn't look like this in high school."

"Well lucky for you I'm not superficial." I leaned in closer.

"So you would have let me take you to the look-out spot to make out."

"I'd have let you feel me up." I placed my hand on his knee. Like this morning at the race, he was wearing shorts. This pair however, were longer than the green ones but it still clung to him in all the right places.

Jamaal's focus dropped to my lips. "And I would have enjoyed every minute of it."

"If you play your cards right maybe you'll get a chance to feel me up tonight." I was feeling bold and I wanted him to know exactly where I hoped this night would lead.

"Don't go messing around issuing checks your ass can't cash."

"I'm not playing. I want to fulfill all of your high school fantasies." I had him hooked and I didn't intend to let go.

The tenor of his voice and the glint in his eye intensified. Jamaal placed a firm hand on the back of my neck. "I want you to suck it, ride it, and take it. No questions asked."

My jaw dropped and an audible gasp escaped my throat. All I had to say to that was, slurp, giddy up, and harder. "How much longer is this cruise?

"About another hour or so."

"Okay, one hour I can handle that."

"There's also the thirty-minute drive back to my place."

I was finding it difficult to breathe, and the center of my panties was saturated with my juices. Fidgeting with my star shaped necklace, I tried to divine a way to push us through time. From the minute he walked into the new hire orientation in his green sweater, slacks, and loafers looking like a sexy professor, I was hooked. I remember sitting with rapt attention, listening to him speak about phishing and ransomware.

While he talked to the new recruits, I studied every inflection, the uptick of an eyebrow, and the subtle smirk that crept over his face when he made a joke about cloud computing. He talked with his hands and I imagined their strength. Something I no longer had to wonder about because the formidable grip he had on my neck let me know he was more than capable of pinning me down while laying the pipe.

"I'm so happy we decided to do this," I said.

"You have no idea." He kissed my cheek, prompting my face to flush.

"Jamaal ..." I tugged on his shirt, giving him a playful shake. "This is light weight torture."

"The cruise?"

"The waiting."

"I waited three months for you to notice me. What's a few more hours?"

To learn that all this time I was crushing on Jamaal and he was secretly crushing on me made me like him even more. Time was a construct strung together by our memories. Fuck the past, present, and future. All that mattered was us and right now.

⸻

Back at Jamaal's apartment, I was face to face with the largest assortment of constructed Lego sets. "Did you do all this?"

"Umm yeah. I warned you I was a nerd." He placed the sneakers I'd kicked off into a cubby near the front door.

"Yeah, but I don't think I grasped the magnitude," I teased.

"You have trouble running uphill and you're judging me?"

I leaned in to examine the items in the custom glass case. "Is that a motorcycle?"

He stood behind me. The heat radiating off his body made it hard to concentrate. "Yes, the BMW M 1000 RR."

"And the Millennium Falcon."

"That's kind of a must have for any Lego collector.

"Lego collector?" I chuckled, spinning on my heels to face him.

"So you're just going to make fun of me for the next fifteen minutes?"

"No. I think it's amazing. You spent time carefully crafting all these items. It's not nerdy. I mean it is. But that's what I like the most about you."

"That I'm a nerd."

"No, that you're true to yourself. You're smart and detail oriented and you don't hide it."

Surveying his space, it was exactly what I'd expect for Jamaal. Clean and organized with a thoughtful design aesthetic. It was clear his furniture was not from the local Ikea like mine. The coffee table was solid wood. They didn't make shit like that anymore and if you found someone who did, it would cost you. His couch was large and roomy, perfect for a movie night or a full on sexcapade. "I like your place. It feels like you."

"Thanks, I like it too. I tend to be a bit of a homebody and I think your home should be your safe haven."

"I like that. My place is more Simone's style than me. The apartment was already furnished when I moved in. Now my bedroom is all me."

"What does all you look like?" He grabbed my hand, removing the many rings adorning my fingers one by one.

"Bright colors and cozy. You'd probably hate it."

Jamaal moved on to my ears, gently unlatching my hoop earrings. "I like bright colors. I'll bring the basics and you'll bring the splash of character."

"Could be a good mix."

"It would be an excellent union." He added my jewelry to a ceramic dish on a nearby side table. "Do you mind if I kiss you?"

"Yes ... I mean no I don't mind. Yes, please kiss away."

He leaned in and planted the most self-assured kiss against my lips. I tossed my arms over his shoulders and inched upward on my toes to deepen our connection. Our feet moved clumsily in the direction of his couch. When his hand slid up my thigh, I was thankful I'd opted for a dress that allowed for immediate skin-on-skin contact. My brain was a laundry list of all the things

I wanted to do to him and every filthy thing I wanted from him in return.

"Is this okay?" It was a question that didn't require an answer, but I nodded in agreement.

Jamaal's hands slipped further up the skirt of my dress. With his thumbs he hooked the string of my thong over my ass and down my thighs. He didn't stop there. Bringing my underwear to his mouth, he licked the sticky wetness from the seat before tossing them aside. My knees buckled as I collapsed to the couch. He positioned himself so he could kiss my knees and the sides of my outer thighs.

Spreading my legs apart, he kissed my inner thighs and I cooed as his lips suckled my sensitive skin. Jamaal's head disappeared under my skirt. I could feel his warm breath inches from my bud teasing me. When he finally touched down with a single swipe, I cried out. I'd been sitting on ready for a hot minute and now that his lips were touching mine, I was turnt. My hips had a mind of their own and moved back and forth, wanting to be fucked by his tongue.

His full lips grabbed hold of my clit and commenced sucking and flicking and I became possessed. My body gyrated and I may have started speaking in tongues because the words I uttered were foreign to my ear. I tugged at the skirt of my dress, lifting it toward me so I could get a better view of what he was doing. The sight of him enjoying me only heightened my pleasure. My hands landed on my breasts and I massaged my nipples over the fabric but it wasn't enough.

"I need to be naked," I announced.

Jamaal pulled away, the lower half of his face shiny as I dripped from his lips. "Okay. I'm not going to complain."

I pulled my dress over my head as he regarded me with eager eyes. Unhooking my bra, I tossed it aside. Jamaal grabbed for me, pulling me down onto him and claiming my left breast in his mouth. As he manipulated my nipple in his mouth, my hand drifted to my center and I rubbed my fingers over my clit. When he realized what I was doing, he pulled back and just admired me as I worked myself into a frenzy.

"Can this be a group assignment?" he finally asked.

"Yes please."

Lowering me back to the couch, Jamaal slid his fingers inside while I worked my tender bud. He never took his eyes off me, marveling at the excellence of our tag team pussy bang. At some point I was no longer a useful team member as my body began to glitch and my eyes retreated to the back of my head. Lucky for me Jamaal picked up the slack, finishing me off with his tongue on my clit and his fingers inside of me.

"Fuck you," I screamed out as an orgasm ripped through my body. I rocked my hips against his mouth, not wanting to miss out on a single drop. Jamaal released my body, still shivering as I came down from my high. Or maybe it was the fact Jamaal's hands were alternating massaging my neck and breast.

I pulled the hair tie from my wrist and secured my braids into a ponytail. "I'm ready to return the favor." Resting my hand on his lap, the expression on my face could only be described as voracious.

10

WINNIE STRIPPED ME OUT OF MY CLOTHES AND MY DICK popped up like a Jack-in-the-box. She was now positioning herself in between my legs. I'd imagined Winnie naked and dripping on all fours before. But nothing I could imagine was sexier than the real thing. Her mahogany skin was flawless. I especially liked her breasts. They fit in my mouth like a puzzle piece and when her nipples grew taut and pert against my tongue, it drove me wild. There was also her perfect ass which I was now regretting I didn't pay more attention to. Next time, I assured myself.

Her delicate hand reached for me and I seeped in a breath of air. Starting at the bottom of my shaft, she planted kisses to my skin. She alternated between a sweet peck, a rolling lick, and a brief suckle until she reached the tip. When she took the tip of my dick in her mouth, I dug my fingers into a nearby couch pillow with a death grip. I witnessed in awe as she made my member disappear deeper down her throat. With my dick slick and wet, she rotated her hands over my lower shaft while swiping her tongue across the top. I eked out a series of grunts and groans.

Winnie lifted her head and smiled at me, licking at the corners of her mouth. "Is everything okay up there?"

I couldn't even offer a polite response. All I could muster was a nod as I pushed her head back toward my member. Winnie was vocal slurping and moaning over me. The sounds that escaped from her throat turned me on. Her soft satisfied groans as she licked me like a popsicle. The gurgling sounds she emitted while trying to take more of me into her mouth.

I stood, needing more control. Placing my hand on the back of her head, I gently guided her over my shaft. Winnie reached upward, dragging her fingers over my chest before settling on the dip in my hips.

"Look at me," I begged.

Caressing her face between licks, she looked up at me with doe-like eyes. As she slid my dick deeper, still the look in her eyes was anything but innocent. Winnie sucked me off like it was her job. She dropped lower and swallowed my balls into her mouth while stroking my shaft, never breaking eye contact. When she finally enveloped me back into her mouth, she performed this twisting suction motion that turned my legs to jelly.

"I'm about to come," I warned her so she could pull away.

"I want to taste you. Is that alright?" she said, quickly before teasing my tip.

Is that alright? I liked Winnie a lot but that was the stupidest question ever asked. You want to suck me until I pour my ecstasy down your throat. That is always okay. My dick trembled and pumped in her mouth. As I released, her moans mixed with mine, a sign we both enjoyed the moment. Winnie pulled me out and focused on the tip, sucking every last drop. I dropped to the floor, no longer able to bear my weight. Reaching for her, I kissed her lips before planting kisses on her cheek and shoulder.

"Are you hungry?" I asked.

"Famished." She smiled.

With one last kiss, I headed to the bathroom to clean up. When I returned to the living room, Winnie was laying on the floor with a content expression on her face. My dick took shape in my basketball shorts, ready for more. But I was starving and the tapas from the boat ride were not enough fuel for me to properly blow her back out. I handed her my MIT T-shirt and entered the kitchen.

"Will grilled cheese work?" I asked. "I think I also have some tomato soup."

Winnie hummed in agreement. Finally rising from the floor and disappearing into the bathroom. When she returned, she was wearing my shirt. Damn that shirt never looked so good and when she raised her arms, I could see a hint of butt cheeks.

"Can I help?"

"Yeah, can you grab the butter from the fridge?"

She retrieved the butter, setting it next to the stove before standing behind me and kissing the muscles in my back.

"Winn, I like everything you're doing right now but I need to eat."

"Fine, you cook and I'll molest you." Her hand slipped into my shorts and she claimed hold of my dick with slow strokes.

My back leaned into her, practically melting. "Please." The plea was for her to stop and not stop in the same breath.

I found her lips kissing her with a moan. Winnie milked me dry until I creamed my shorts. Removing her hand, she licked me from her fingers, an act that made me want to bend her over the counter and give her the business. Instead, I grabbed her by the shoulders and moved her to the other side of the kitchen counter. After cleaning up for a second time, I returned to the kitchen and successfully finished making the grilled cheese sandwiches and warming up the soup. Sitting in the bar stool next to her, we dug in.

"This is good," Winnie said around a bite.

"Thank you." I had one hand on my sandwich and the other caressing the back of her neck. "Do you have plans for Sunday?" I asked.

"Tomorrow? No ... Sundays are usually the day I clean and meal prep. What about you?"

"I was hoping, maybe you'd want to spend the day together."

"Hmm ... let me think. House chores or guaranteed sex." She raised and lowered her hands like a scale.

"So that's a yes."

"There will be sex ... right?"

"Yes," I licked my lips before giving her a sloppy kiss.

"Then count me in."

Surprisingly, Winnie lived up to the hype. She was just as amazing as I'd built her up to be in my head. On more than one occasion, I'd gotten ahead of my skis, falling for the illusion of what a relationship could be and not what clearly was. But Winnie felt like the real deal. She was smart, kind, and funny. And we hadn't even had full on intercourse yet and I was already mentally making room for her things in the closet.

"Great it's a sleepover."

"I loved sleepovers when I was a kid. Granted it just meant sleeping in a different RV or trailer, but it was the best. Popcorn, sweet snacks, and movies."

"That sounds like a hell of a night."

"Just means you have big shoes to fill. Because past sleepovers have been epic."

"I think I have some ideas on how to make this night memorable."

Winnie's lips curved into a naughty grin. "I'd like to hear some of them."

Slipping my hand into hers, I said, "Well first we need to get out of —"

We were interrupted by a knock at the door, followed by the buzz of the doorbell. It was well after midnight, and I wasn't expecting any guests. I reluctantly untwisted myself from Winnie's arms. At the door, I looked through the peephole and Miles was standing on the other side. Rushing back into the living room, I collected our clothes and tossed them into my bedroom.

"Who is it?" Winnie gasped. "Oh my God, is it your mother?"

"No?" my forehead wrinkled in confusion.

"Is it your girlfriend?" Her voice took on a high panicked pitch.

I stopped in my tracks and stared her in the eye. "No. Don't be silly. I'm trying to make *you* my girlfriend."

Her face lit up and she twisted one of her braids through her fingers. The knocking at the door persisted. Grabbing Winnie by the hand, I pulled her to the bedroom. In my dresser, I located a pair of shorts with a drawstring and tossed them to her before closing the bedroom door.

Heading back to the front door, I opened it with a grimace. "Do you have any idea what time it is?"

"What? When we were younger we would just be leaving for the club right about now."

"We are not younger."

"Speak for yourself, old man." Miles pushed past me. "What took you so long to answer the door?" His head swiped over my meticulously neat place and landed on the two plates and cups on the kitchen counter. "Do you have company?"

"What do you want, Miles?"

"Damn can't a man just want to spend some quality time with his best friend?"

"Let me guess your supermodel was busy."

Miles heeled his shoes off, letting me know he intended to stay awhile. "Why are you being so rude? Did I come at a bad time?"

"Yes you did. And if you'd called or texted beforehand I could have told you that."

My bedroom door opened and Winnie poked her head out. "Do I have to stay in here?" she asked. Her big curious eyes landed on Miles and I think both their jaws dropped in unison.

Miles's head whipped round in my direction, his open mouth turning into a smirk. "Are you two—"

"What are you doing here?" Winnie asked, joining us in the living room.

"What are *you* doing here?" Miles lobbed her question back at her.

I pointed at Winnie. "So ... funny story. Miles is my cousin." I smiled at her sheepishly.

"Play cousin?" she asked.

"Blood cousin. Our mothers are sisters," I answered.

Winnie's gaze pinged from my face to Miles and back again as if she was noticing the resemblance in real time. "Let me get this straight, you work at the IT help desk of the Fortune 500 company your cousin owns?"

"IT help desk?" Miles let out a disrespectful chuckle.

I flashed him the look of death and he quickly fell silent. "It's a little more complicated than that but we can discuss it later."

"Maybe I should leave," Winnie said, backing toward the bedroom.

"No, you're my guest and I want you to stay." Turning to Miles, my tone was gruff. "What the fuck do you want?"

"Shit I'm over here going through an existential crisis and come to you for advice and this is how you treat me?"

"What's wrong?" Winnie's voice was laced with concern.

"Thank you. Thank you, Winifred for caring." Miles placed his hand over his heart.

I hissed out a breath. "Okay what's the problem this time? Are you torn between purchasing the high-rise penthouse in Chicago or the modest nine bedroom estate in Belmore?"

"No, I'd just buy them both. Real estate is a great investment." Miles made himself comfortable in the armchair next to the couch. "Do you think we could get some tea going? I always feel better when I have something warm in my tummy."

"Umm, yeah. I can make some tea," Winnie offered.

"No, you're off duty. You do not have to cater to my cousin on your day off. I'll make the tea."

"I don't mind."

"I do," I said, heading to the kitchen with Winnie close on my heels.

"You seem agitated. Are you and Miles not on good terms?"

"I'm fine. Never been better. My cousin needs attention and we all just have to drop everything to massage the ego of a man-child."

Winnie's eyes took up her full face.

Resting my hand on her arm, I reassured her it was alright. "I just wanted tonight to be about you and me. But it seems like Miles inserts himself into everything at work, at home." Clearing my throat, I added, "It doesn't matter. I'm used to playing second fiddle."

Miles's voice echoed from the living room. "You two do know I can hear you right? And I'm not a man-child. I'm a sensitive soul."

With a belly of green tea, Miles rambled unfettered about Codeability and the pressures of running a company that size. "This afternoon I was on a tech panel with some of the brightest minds in the industry. All making moves in their own right. And I felt like I didn't belong. So much so that I almost had a mini panic attack on the stage. I feel like every interview, magazine article, conference, I'm just waiting for someone to escort me from the room informing me there's been a mistake and I'm not supposed to be there." Miles dropped his head into his hands.

"There's a term for what you're feeling," Winnie said. "Have you ever heard of imposter syndrome?"

"No, what's that? Is it some type of disease? Do I have a disease?" Miles's already distressed voice was elevating in pitch.

"It's not a disease. It's psychological."

"That explains a lot," I quipped.

Winnie swatted my arm. "Essentially, it's when highly capable and intelligent people experience success but feel like they are undeserving. They fear that eventually everyone will find out they're a fraud."

"Hmm," I groaned.

Winnie continued, "It doesn't matter how smart they are or the fact that they earned their seat at the table. They just never feel worthy."

"That's it. I don't feel worthy of the success and accolades."

"Maybe you feel that way because you're *not* deserving."

Winnie's eyes slammed into me. "Jamaal."

"Sorry just playing devil's advocate. Offering an opposing view." I raised my hands in surrender.

"Miles has worked really hard to build Codeability from the ground up, of course he's worthy of the accolades and financial rewards."

"Of course, what was I thinking?" I said.

Miles locked eyes with me and without words, we communicated multitudes of hurt feelings and old wounds we'd agreed to let go of because we were family. He was lucky Winnie was here to act as a buffer. My cousin knew his success was a sore subject for me partly because it wasn't earned, it was stolen.

"Imposter Syndrome is very common for Black and Brown people who operate in predominantly White spaces. I could Google some daily affirmations to help when the negative thoughts creep in."

My jaw clenched at the thought of Winnie overextending herself for a man who would never really appreciate it.

"You'd do that for me?" Miles's eyes grew wide in admiration.

"Of course. You're Jamaal's cousin." She grabbed hold of my hand, giving it a squeeze. "Anything to help."

"Team player." He snapped his fingers at us. "You two are a perfect couple. So tell me everything. How long has this been going on?" Miles crossed his arms, waiting for us to dish.

"It's late. I'm sure you have some party to attend."

"I did get invited to the XYZ Baby party. I'm not really a fan of his music but the women at his parties are top tier. Do you like XYZ Baby?"

Winnie shook her head. "No, he's kind of a misogynistic asshole."

Miles let out a robust laugh. "He really is the worst."

I stood up, signaling the end of the conversation. "Thanks so much for stopping by."

"Are you coming to dinner tomorrow?" Miles asked

"I'll try to make it. Your parents are hosting right?"

"Yep, bring Winifred. Aunt Phyllis would love her."

Absolutely the fuck not. The relationship was new. I was trying to convince Winnie I was a good catch, not trying to outline all the reasons I wasn't. My family, though well intentioned, would embarrass the shit out of me.

Finding his feet, Miles reached for Winnie's hand, planting a kiss. "Thank you for listening. I appreciate it, seriously."

"Of course."

Miles slipped into his shoes and I walked him to the door. "Are you mad at me?" he asked.

"No Miles. Why would I be mad at you?"

"Jamaal if you still feel a way about—"

"It's late. I'm tired. Nothing more."

That wasn't entirely true. But I did not want to rehash the past and listen to Miles regurgitate the same old excuses. Plus, Winnie was here, and she didn't need to witness Miles and I cuss each other out.

11

TODAY WAS FULL OF SURPRISES. BUT FINDING OUT Jamaal and Miles were related was a shocker. I would've never guessed. And Miles never mentioned it. Not that he would. He barely talked to me. And when he did, it was always a request. Copy this, fetch that, throw this away. You'd think I'd have heard something through my connections from the office grapevine. But stories about Jamaal and Miles hadn't made it to the mail room.

When Jamaal returned to the living room, his expression was marred with irritation.

"Everything okay?"

"Yeah, peachy." Jamaal gathered my hands in his. "Look, Winn I was going to tell you about Miles."

"Eventually?"

"Yeah, I just don't typically lead with that information."

"Am I the only one who doesn't know you two are related?"

"No, no one knows. I told Risha but no one else at Code-ability knows. It's not a secret, it's just not relevant."

"Hmm ... but it kind of is."

"Does my cousin being CEO change things between us?"

"No. But I just wish you felt comfortable trusting me with your secrets."

"To be fair we're still in the getting to know you stage. But if you want to know all my dirty little secrets, here they are. I sleep with a mouth guard because I grind my teeth. I didn't lose my virginity until I was twenty. And my parents are well off."

We would definitely circle back to the news of Miles's silver spoon childhood. But I was more concerned with the subtle pressure that filled the room upon Miles's arrival. "What's the deal with you and Miles?"

"How do you mean?"

"I sensed tension."

"It's nothing, we're family. Cousins tend to butt heads. But we love each other." He clenched his teeth and I witnessed the muscles in his jaw ruminate.

"I get being annoyed. My cousin Chris loves to tease me about my long toes." Jamaal's eyes were immediately drawn to my bare feet. I curled my digits, hoping to conceal the length. "Anyway, he was always calling me bigfoot and claiming God mixed up and gave me two set of hands."

The edges of Jamaal's mouth began to curve upward.

I pointed a finger of warning in his direction. "If you laugh—"

"I'm not laughing. Kids can be cruel."

"He's well into his thirties and makes the same lame jokes every time I see him."

"Your toes look ... normalish to me."

"This isn't about my feet. I just want to let you know I'm a good listener. And it seemed like you were biting your tongue the entire time Miles was here."

"We don't always see eye to eye."

"Why?" I moved to the couch, giving the empty space next to me a pat.

Sitting, he offered up a blasé shrug.

"Jamaal?" I squeezed his hand, hoping he'd share. It was clear something was weighing on him.

Expelling a long hiss-like breath, he said, "He stole Codeability from me. The idea, the initial code, the business plan. All of it."

"Oh my God." I understood the words, but was still unsure of what it all meant. Miles was touted as a genius and a change maker. So hearing Jamaal say all of the innovation was stolen and Miles was a great big phony, was unexpected. And maybe that played into the imposter syndrome Miles was feeling because all the praise and adulation he received was unearned.

"Yeah." He sank further into the couch cushions.

"Why are you working there?" Jamaal's expression grew cautious. "I don't mean that in an accusatory way, more in the sense of how can you stand to see him profit off of your ideas?"

"Miles is like a brother to me. I looked up to him. I trusted him. And in the end I just decided to believe the theft wasn't malicious. We're blood, something like this would have torn our family apart."

"So you helped him create your dream?"

"What Codeability ended up becoming resembles what I created. But at some point he had to figure it out on his own because I was no longer willing to share my ideas with him. So Codeability is a bastardized version of what I envisioned."

"What I don't get is the audacity. He steals your company and then hires you on as IT support."

Jamaal clicked his tongue and his mouth was arranged in a sour line.

"What?"

"Actually, my job title is Director of Application Development."

Bewilderment unhitched my jaw.

"I can explain."

"Quickly."

"You *assumed* I was the IT guy."

"You never corrected me."

"Because I had a crush on you. And seeing your face was the highlight of my day."

His words settled in my core like a sip of honey blossom tea. That was one of the sweetest things anyone had said to me. I don't think anyone had ever paid particular attention to my coming and goings. Once I owned a hamster that would squeal every time I returned to the RV, so I guess that could count. "This night has been like a reality show reunion. Surprise guest, secrets revealed, sex."

"Close your legs to married men." He quoted a line from a popular reality housewives show hand gestures included and we both dissolved into laughter.

When Jamaal confessed he wasn't the IT guy I probably in turn should have admitted I wasn't a bumbling tech idiot and that the sticky caps key was courtesy of a little nail glue. *Don't look at me like that. Not all of my technology issues were man-made, a few were just dumb luck.* At the end of the day, we both told a few off white or beige lies to get closer to one another. The intentions were coming from a positive place and that's really all that mattered.

"Is Miles going to tell anyone about us?"

"Nah, he wouldn't do that." Jamaal glanced at me from the corner of his eye. "If he did would that be a problem?"

"I don't want people getting the wrong impression."

"Which would be what? That we're a couple?" I loved the way his hands always found a part of my body to fixate on. Right now, his fingers were tickling the skin just behind my left ear.

"Are we a couple?"

"Would it be strange if I said yes?"

"I've heard stranger things."

"Like?"

"The fact that killer whales can only stay submerged underwater for fifteen minutes before they have to come up for air. Which doesn't really make sense because they live in water." When I was nervous, I was a walking Wikipedia.

"I did not know that." His hand was now making circles on my thigh.

"Most people don't."

"So tell me this. How long have you been pining after me?" he teased.

My face grew flush as I chuckled. "I don't think you remember this, but I first saw you in an IT training class for all the newbies."

"I remember I kept getting distracted by your smile."

And just like that my goofy smile made an appearance. It was sweet but there was no way I stood out in a room full of close to a hundred people. "Shut up."

"No, I'm serious. Hand to God I'm a better presenter than that. I don't usually stutter and trip over my words. But I just kept trying to think of something witty I could say during a break to get your attention."

"You should have said hi. I can guarantee you that would've worked."

"About halfway through, I'd already determined you were out of my league and I needed to hang it up."

"Me? Pfft."

"You were wearing a yellow sweater with embroidered purple and green flowers on the shoulders. Half of your braids were pinned back from your face." He collected a handful of my hair, replicating the look. "When you ate the snacks in your new hire tote bag, you danced in your seat like it was the best food ever. And when you stopped to thank me for the training afterward, you reminded me of the flowers in my parent's backyard at full bloom. All I could think about was you—" His last words trailed off as he claimed my lips.

My mouth ticked up into a smile, so happy to be back in his arms. His strong hands cupped the back of my neck as if he wanted to lock me into this distinct moment in time. I had no intention of going anywhere except to the bed with this delightful man. Sweet, humble, and thoughtful men were hard to find, and Jamaal possessed those qualities in spades.

"I need you," he moaned against my lips.

"I'm all yours," I professed.

He stood, leading me to his room. In silence, we shed our clothes. My body trembled in excitement for him. Jamaal retrieved a condom from a ceramic box on his nightstand. With the condom in place, he sat on the bench at the foot of his bed. Pulling me close, he planted kisses to my backside and thighs. He then guided me onto his lap, my chest pressed against his.

Hooking my legs over his, I spread myself wide open. With his hands on my waist, I lifted my bottom before slowly lowering myself onto his stiff dick. I gasped softly as he filled me completely. Our bodies moved in harmony with each other. Jamaal's hand cupped my breast, his thumb rubbing my nipple.

"Does that feel good? I want to make you feel good," he asked.

"Yes, you feel so good," I managed to choke out.

My eyes rolled to the back of my head from a satisfying thrust. He found my lips and we exchanged sloppy fuck me kisses. Slurping, sucking, licking. Jamaal grabbed my ass, guiding me up and down his shaft and the intensity of the strokes forced me to cry out. You ever play Dance Dance Revolution where you have to move and hit various combinations to get a high score? That was Jamaal right now. His perfectly timed strokes were unlocking new levels and placing him on top of the leaderboard of past lovers.

"Jamaal, baby please." My breath hitched and sputtered.

"Breathe baby. Breathe for me."

I exhaled a shaky breath. My eyes were locked onto his. He was so beautiful and his only objective was making me come. When his hand landed on my honey pot, I felt lightheaded. "I think I'm going to faint. It's too much." Listen I was coming off of months without sex or physical touch to being fondled with all my nerve endings firing at the same time. I wasn't no punk, I could take the dick, but the euphoria was making me a smidge lightheaded.

"Do you want me to stop?"

"No, please don't stop." Leaning into him with deep kisses and his hands all over me was a level of intimacy I'd crave for a long time. He was fucking me but it was laced with a care and respect I couldn't explain. It was as if everything he did was in service of me. His pleasure was secondary.

Jamaal's lips coasted over my neck and he sucked hard. I didn't care. "Brand me, baby. I want everyone to know I'm yours." This one position with our limbs entangled was all I needed. Jamaal slid his thumb in my mouth and I worked my tongue around it as the rest of his digits caressed the side of my cheek.

"Fuck Winnie," he groaned in my ear.

My body was on fire as I rocked my hips in a circle. When the first wave of ecstasy hit, I tensed from head to toe followed by shivers and the pulsating throb of my pussy tightening around him. Jamaal enveloped me in his arms and bit into my shoulder, the sharp pain making me come harder.

He grunted low before yelling, "Gotdamnit Winn." Now it was his turn to convulse and shake.

We collapsed onto the bed trying to regain our composure. Jamaal reached for my hand, bringing it to his lips for a kiss.

"You're perfect," he said.

I turned toward him. "Don't do that. Nobody's perfect. You'll end up disappointed."

"Let me rephrase. You are perfectly imperfect, and I like everything about you."

My smile was cautious. I wanted to believe that this time it was real. That the flutter in my stomach was butterflies and not wasps. I'd read somewhere that all humans had a baseline of happiness. Meaning no matter how much your life improved ... new car, promotion, finding the love of your life, eventually we all leveled out and returned to our happiness baseline. My fear was that when the new pussy smell wore off, Jamaal would return to his baseline and no longer be as enamored by Winnie Chambers from Everywhere, USA.

After spending all weekend with Jamaal, Monday came far too soon. It had been hours since we'd been together, but my body was still responding to the memory of him. On the drive to work, my lady parts contracted as I played back our rendezvous. At my desk, I was greeted by an arrangement of flowers. Not any ordinary flowers, this bouquet was made out of Legos. The vase was real; everything else was a Lego piece in vibrant pink, purple and yellow hues. I retrieved the card attached to the vase and it read.

TO WINN:

THE FLOWERS MAY BE FAKE, BUT MY FEELINGS FOR YOU ARE VERY REAL. THANK YOU FOR MAKING THIS A MEMORABLE WEEKEND.
WITH APPRECIATION,
JAMAAL, FROM IT.

I couldn't conceal the smile spreading across my face. Pressing the card to my nose it reminded me of his earthy citrus essence. The scent triggered my center to activate, dampening my thong. Tucking the card in my purse, I powered up my computer before heading to the executive kitchenette to put together a tray of pastries and start a pot of coffee for Miles's first meeting of the day.

Miles wasn't in the office often, but when he was, his days were usually packed with meetings. In the conference room, I set the tray on the table and then set off on pressing various buttons that turned on lights and opened window coverings. This wasn't part of my duties, but since I'd gotten an earlier start unable to sleep last night, partly because I missed Jamaal, I decided to help the receptionist out.

I actually preferred the office when it was empty and quiet like this. For most of the day, it was nonstop chatter with staff coming in and out with documents requiring signatures, or questions that just couldn't wait. At this early hour, I didn't have to be pleasant or accommodating and I could focus on knocking out tasks in peace.

"My opinion holds weight and has value to others," a deep voice called from behind me.

I released a blood-curdling scream before quickly reaching for a stapler to launch at the intruder's head.

"Winifred, it's me ... Miles. I was just quoting one of the affirmations you emailed over." His hands were raised in surrender.

"You scared the shit out of me and you almost got pegged in the face with this stapler." It was barely seven o'clock, most employees didn't start showing up until nine. I was under the assumption I was all alone. Clearing my throat, I regained my composure. "Sorry about the cussing."

Miles walked deeper into the office space. "It's all good. I mean we are practically family."

"I don't know about all that."

"I know my cousin and the way he was looking at you the other night. I give it six months before you're sporting a ring or a baby bump. Because one does not need a marriage to have a fulfilling romantic relationship. At least that's what I keep telling my mother."

I gave into a gentle laugh. Before this weekend, I would've placed heavy odds against Miles knowing my name. He rarely spoke to me. Even when we were in the same room it was like I was invisible. Now he knew my name and that I was fucking his cousin, and I knew his dirty little secret as well.

"What did Jamaal say about me after I left?" he asked, propping himself on a nearby desk.

"What others think of me is not my problem. The only thoughts I can control are my own. That was another affirmation you may have missed in that email I sent you." If Miles expected me to betray Jamaal's confidence, he was sorely mistaken.

Miles scoffed before moving on. "Why are you here so early?"

"Couldn't sleep."

"Normally when I can't sleep, I go for a run or a walk."

"Well, I hate running and historically for women running in the early morning when the streets are deserted can be dangerous."

"Right ... sorry. I didn't think about that. Well since you're here can you make me that chocolate and banana smoothie I like?"

It would appear the tranquility was over. I deposited the remaining stack of handouts I'd been setting out in the conference room on my desk. "I'll get on that right away."

"Winifred, I was joking. I'm more than capable of making my own smoothie."

"Jokes are typically funny."

"Ouch. I see why he likes you. Jamaal has always had great taste in women."

I stared at him blankly.

"Not that there's been a ton of women. I'm not saying he's some type of player."

"Maybe you should quit while you're ahead."

"Noted."

"And I have no issues with making your smoothie."

"That would be great because honestly, I suck at making them. They're either too watered down or too chunky."

After making his drink, I found Miles in his office scrolling on his phone. I set the smoothie on a coaster in front of him with a glass straw and extra napkins just like I was trained on my first week on the job. Jerrika told me Miles was fussy and liked things just so, and if I didn't get it right the first time, it would be my last time.

I turned to leave, hoping to finish up my morning routine.

"Winifred, thanks for the affirmations. I don't know if it'll help but I do appreciate it." He never looked up from his phone.

"You're welcome."

Following his morning meeting, Jerrika and I met with Miles to go over his calendar and solidify plans for the next few weeks. My role was mostly that of a silent scribe. Once we penciled in upcoming speaking engagements, Miles turned to us and asked, "Do you think Friday's event went well?

"Yes," Jerrika chimed in. "Employees were happy, the food and drink vendors were delicious, and everyone had a good time."

"What about me? Do you think my little speech helped with morale?"

"Employees love to hear from you. The turnout was huge because they knew you were going to be in attendance."

Miles made his way over to the wall of windows in his office overlooking the campus. "Do you think I should be doing more? I feel like the bigger this company gets the harder it is to connect with the staff. It's not like it was in the beginning when there were ten team members and I knew everyone's names."

Jerrika nodded. "Well that's a good point ... maybe—"

Miles turned toward me. "Winifred, what are your thoughts?"

It was very much like being thrust into the spotlight. I was so used to being seen and not heard that I practically choked on my tongue. Jerrika eyed me, awaiting my response. She liked to limit my communications with Miles. It was all in an effort to gatekeep entry into his good graces. God forbid he compliment my work or agree with an idea I shared. If Miles hadn't insisted I attend these planning meetings, I'm sure Jerrika would've iced me out a long time ago.

Taking a deep breath, I selected my next words carefully. "I can understand the desire to get back to the early days when everyone on the team was invested in the company's success. With the massive growth Codeability has seen in recent years it can be difficult to navigate, but I think there are opportunities for engagement—"

"Thanks for the reminder, Winnie," Jerrika interrupted. "Miles I'd been meaning to talk to you about ways you can have a greater impact on the staff. My thought is Meals with Miles ..."

My jaw unhinged hitting the floor like a cartoon character as I listened to Jerrika pitch *my* idea to Miles. The same idea I'd mentioned last week that she aggressively shut down. *This fucking bitch.* I wanted to jump from my seat and shift her wig. I'm talking about a WWE style smackdown. But I didn't. I just sat there thunderstruck, while she brazenly claimed my idea as her own.

"I don't hate it. Maybe it would be good to mix it up and get up close and personal with the people that help Codeability run," Miles said.

At this point I was shooting dagger eyes in Jerrika's direction, but she knew better than to make eye contact with me. If she had, the rage in my eyes would've turned her to ash. After we were dismissed Jerrika hightailed it to the elevator, most likely to avoid being confronted by me. Honestly, I didn't even know what I would say to her. I hated conflict, rarely ever speaking up for myself. I'd taken shit on the chin for so long it now had a permanent indentation. In the kitchen I made myself a mocha latte with extra whipped cream, hoping to drown my rising irritation in sugary sweet nirvana.

My phone chimed with a message from Jamaal.

Jamaal: Dinner tonight? My place.

Winnie: Yes, and I'm going to need some strong drinks to go along with it.

Jamaal: Uh-oh, what's up?

Winnie: I'll tell you tonight.

Jamaal: Understood. Is it a Vodka or Hennessy type of night?

Winnie: Hennessy … definitely Hennessy.

12

WINNIE ENTERED MY APARTMENT LIKE A STORM. SHOES kicked off at the entry hall, keys tossed onto a side table, and her purse dropped without a second thought for the random contents which had scattered to the carpet.

"I need a drink now," she announced.

I poured her some Hennessy, handing over the glass.

She took it to the head before gagging and spitting it out. "What the hell is that?"

"It's Hennessy."

"*That's* Hennessy?"

"Have you never had Hennessy?" My eyes climbed my forehead.

"No." She smacked her tongue, trying to eliminate the unpleasant aftertaste.

I massaged my temples. "Then why did you ask for it?"

"Because I'm pissed and it seemed like the right choice. But that shit is disgusting."

"It's an acquired taste for sure. Wine?"

"Yes. I'm a wine girlie. I don't know who I was kidding." After a long sip of red wine, her shoulders seemed to relax. "I missed you." She wrapped her arms around me with kisses that made it difficult to focus. My hand slid to her backside, grabbing a handful of ass. Winnie cupped my face with a sexy pout. I don't know if she intended for it to be sexy, but it was to me. "I wish I'd never gotten out of bed this morning."

"What happened?'

"Jerrika is what happened. We had our monthly scheduling meeting with Miles and Jerrika pitched my idea about Meals with Miles like it was hers. 'Well Miles I did have a thought ...'" Winnie imitated Jerrika's nasally voice. "'It's called Meals with Miles and I think the staff would really appreciate having focused time with you.' That fucking vulture is picking thoughts out of my brain while I'm still alive and kicking." Winnie paced back and forth, her anger increasing with each step.

I pulled my face into an impressed expression. "Wow, that's really a good idea."

"I know right, and she stole it from me like ... like a person who steals things."

"A thief?" I offered.

"Yes, a thief, thank you. I'm so mad I can't think straight."

"She pulled a Miles Graves on you."

"My idea wasn't a billion-dollar one ... but ... yeah she kind of did. I'm several fries short of a Happy Meal right now and I just want to ..." Winnie threw punches at an imaginary figure in front of her. When the jabs slowed, she eyed me shyly. "Sorry."

"No need to apologize. Bosses like Jerrika are the worst."

"It's not even really about Jerrika. She's a duplicitous bitch and I've always known that. I'm just so pissed at myself. You should have seen me. I just sat there and let her steal my idea word for word like a pathetic loser."

"Trust me I get it."

Winnie rested her hand on my folded arms. "You are not a pathetic loser. Your situation with Miles is totally different. You guys are family."

I shrugged. "So what are you going to do about Jerrika?"

"What can I do?" Winnie's shoulders rounded into a heap. "This isn't the first idea she's stolen and it won't be her last."

"You can call her out on her bullshit."

"I can't, she's my boss." Winnie tugged at the collar of her shirt.

"She's a crappy leader who doesn't want her employee to shine."

"And she's never had an original thought to save her life. She could've at least said it was our idea. Why did she feel the need to take all the credit for something she didn't even think of?"

"I'm not certain but I think it may go back to her being a selfish bitch."

"I feel trapped. Jerrika's never going to change and she's never going to allow me to grow outside of my very specific role of coffee gofer."

"If you let her get away with this it'll never end. She'll just keep stealing your great ideas and claiming them as her own."

"You're right. I can't ignore this. I've peeped her game and I'm not the one to play with."

"You need to let her know in no uncertain terms all the ways she's got you fucked up."

"I get it, we're Black in corporate America which means we have to be ten times brighter than everyone else, go above and beyond, and never be seen as the angry Black Negro. But sometimes you have to let people who fucked around find out."

"And if you get fired—"

"Wait, you think I could get fired?"

"I mean ... Jerrika sounds like a petty person."

Winnie's eyes grew wide. "I can't get fired Jamaal, I have sixty dollars in my savings account."

I cringed.

"Maybe I should just let it go."

"Look I've got your back no matter what you do. And if you do get fired I can float you some cash for a few months."

"Jamaal, I don't take handouts. I'm perfectly capable of supporting myself."

"Okay, but the sixty dollars in your bank account says different," I teased.

"I need food and another glass of wine. After that I'll be able to think clearer."

After dinner I had dessert, eating Winnie out before fucking her to sleep. I peered up at her, teasing her nipples while I pleased her clit. The way her legs shook before boxing me between her thighs put a smile on my face. Her pussy looked like a donut, glazed and cream filled. My fingers slid between her folds, slippery from my spit and her juices. I decided to make it my mission to fuck her cares away.

Winnie's back arched as she rose from the bed. She rocked her hips and I extended my stiff tongue, letting her control the intensity. As she moved, she made sure I licked her clit before sliding upward so I could savor the rest of her. When that orgasm hit, she screamed my name and I beamed with pride, satisfied that I'd satisfied her.

Winnie sunk into the bed, her eyes hooded, her legs wide waiting to receive me. With a condom in place, I entered with little effort. Her shit was like a slip and slide. My strokes were steady and intentional. The goal was for her to feel all of me and the way my body responded to being surrounded by hers. I folded Winnie's agile body like a pretzel, her legs hooked over my shoulders and her bottom in the air. Sweat coasted down my back as I drilled deeper with each thrust, until her voice was hoarse from crying out in rapture.

Removing her legs from my shoulder, I slowed things down with some let's make a baby type moves. Strokes that communicated I thought she was the prettiest, sexiest girl in the whole wide world. After minutes of making love to her with kisses that made me shiver, I pulled my dick out and tapped it on the top of her pussy, hitting her clit with my tip. Winnie moaned and covered her face with a pillow.

I ripped the pillow away. "Don't hide from me," I ordered,

sliding back in place between her thighs. "I want to see your pretty face when you come."

Her brown eyes locked in on mine, intoxicated with lust. It only took a few more thrusts before she was moaning through labored gasps for breath. I was right behind her. She made me come so hard my ears were ringing. After a few lingering kisses, I headed to the bathroom.

It had literally been days, but I was already all in with Winnie. I was a planner, and I was currently trying to decide if she'd be able to move in here with me or if we'd have to get another place. Maybe I should start looking at houses? It was a seller's market. It was safe to say I'd never felt this way about anyone before. When she came over upset about her boss, I had the urge to text Miles and tell him to fire Jerrika.

Miles would do it too. California was an at-will employment state. Winnie wasn't looking to me to fix her problems, she just wanted to vent and talk things through. However, if Jerrika didn't do right by Winnie, her days were numbered. *Whoa, that sounded ominous.* But I could make her disappear ... from the Codeability campus escorted by security with all her things packed in a cardboard box.

When I returned, Winnie was where I'd left her, arms wide welcoming me back to bed.

"Do you own the couch?" I asked.

"What?"

"The couch at your place, is it yours or Simone's?"

"Hers, why?"

I shook my head "No reason, just wondering." Sinking into her arms, I whispered, "Are you feeling better?"

"Yes. Thank you."

"I aim to please."

"Well, you succeeded because I am thoroughly satisfied. Consider me a loyal customer."

"Ooo, being a loyal customer comes with perks."

"Like what?" She brushed her index finger across my cheek.

"Turn around and I'll show you."

Winnie's eyes grew wide but she complied turning on to her stomach. I pulled her ass to the sky and submerged my face between her ass cheeks, my dick coming to life ready for round two.

I was having difficulty sleeping so I left Winnie in the bedroom, dead to the world. Since I couldn't rest, I could use this time to work on my extracurricular project. Opening my laptop, I pulled up various spreadsheets and a PowerPoint presentation. An hour in and the coffee table was a mess with papers filled with code and data.

The bedroom door opened, and Winnie lazily walked to the kitchen, grabbing a glass of water. Reentering the living room, she examined my pile of documents, pens, and markers. She was wearing one of my Codeability T-shirts that was handed out at the company launch party. It had shrunk from being washed so many times and right now was barely covering Winnie's naughty bits.

"Whatcha doing?" she asked.

"I couldn't sleep so I thought I'd work."

"You're working at three in the morning for Codeability?" She plopped next to me on the floor.

"This isn't for Codeability."

Winnie reached for a handful of documents and skimmed through them. "What's Priority Desk?"

"Priority Desk is my new business idea."

"How does it work?"

I looked at her hesitantly. I still bore the scars of what happened the last time I shared my idea with someone.

"You don't have to tell me. It's cool."

Squeezing her knee I said, "Priority Desk is a personal assistant that's available—"

"24/7," she beamed.

"Exactly. We are living in a world where people are willing to pay for convenience. This app allows them to hire their very own personal assistant for the day or for the hour. You have clothes at the dry cleaners but you're too busy or lazy to pick it up. Priority Desk can do it for you. You forgot the garlic cloves for spaghetti night and the kids are sleeping. Go on the app and your personal assistant will pick it up for you. You're stuck at the airport and you need to find a flight after yours has been cancelled. You enter a price range and time frame and your personal assistant does all the rest."

"Just like the rich and famous."

"Just like that but at an affordable rate. Prices will vary on the services. You need someone to pick up Roxy from the groomer? It'll cost ... umm ... forty dollars."

"That's kind of steep."

"I thought so too. But one thing people appreciate is having someone else handle the mundane daily task they dread doing. People will literally spend eighty dollars on a meal that would cost thirty if they picked it up themselves. Why? Because it's convenient. Not having to jump in the car, navigate through traffic, find parking. Have someone else do it at a cost."

"True, I cringe every time I order food from one of those apps, but it's just so damn easy."

I tapped my temple.

"So what is this prospective proposal about?"

"Umm ... I plan to pitch Priority Desk to potential investors in a few weeks."

"Investors to launch the app?"

"Launch the app, secure office space, hire staff."

Winnie turned to face me head on. "Shut the front door. You're going to leave Codeability."

"I don't really know what I'm doing. If I don't get any investors it's all a moot point."

"I thought you liked what you did at the company?"

"I do. But it was never my vision to work for *my* company. I was supposed to run it. Honestly the best thing that came out of working there was meeting you."

Winnie was silent as she took in the mess of papers and file folders.

"You think I'm making a mistake?" What Winnie thought about this was important to me. I wanted her to believe in me. So I wasn't the only one who believed in this dream.

"Do you want me to fix your presentation?" she asked, shaking the printed slide pages.

"What's wrong with the presentation?"

"Visually it could be more succinct. You're going to be pitching to people who may not have the same tech savvy. I could make it more relatable. I do it all the time for some of the other executives before they present to Miles."

"You'd do that?"

"For you, anything. How long do we have?

"A little over a month." I grimaced recognizing that was a lot to ask.

"Leave it to me."

A burst of fizzy warmth traveled through my body. I leaned my head on her shoulder and breathed deep. "Thank you."

13

It was Friday and yes, I'd waited until the end of the week to finally confront Jerrika. But I needed those days in between to calm down. I didn't want to confront Jerrika from a place of rage and come off as the angry Black woman. Truthfully, running from that stereotype is probably what landed me in this predicament. Winnie Chambers always has a smile on her face, willing to pitch in to help anyone even if it wasn't her job.

Like the time I helped the lady who comes each week to water our plants. I found her in the bathroom sobbing her eyes out. In an effort to help, I told her I'd finish up her duties grabbing her watering can and duster. I watered every fiddle fig, fern, and elephant ear plant on the top floor. She did gift me with a succulent arrangement the next week that was still thriving on my desk.

People thought I was a pushover. I wasn't, I was just new and still in observation mode. If Jerrika pushed me, I could set it off like Jada in that one movie that … I … had not seen. I shot Jamaal a quick text telling him to add the heist movie to my list.

It was three in the afternoon and there were no staff events planned this evening because of the three-day weekend.

"Jerrika, can I speak to you …privately?"

"I'm leaving in thirty minutes. I need to head to the airport." Her tone was always so dry. She only showed enthusiasm when talking to the executives.

"Well, this won't take that long."

We used Miles' office for our conversation. He hadn't been in the office since Monday.

"What." She paid more attention to her phone screen than me.

"Okay ... rude," I blurted out.

"Excuse me?"

"Your tone was rude. It's always rude but I didn't bring you in here to discuss the fact that it cost zero dollars to be kind."

Jerrika stared at me, dumbstruck.

"On Monday, you pitched Miles an idea that wasn't yours."

"What are you talking about?"

"Meals with Miles. You pitched my idea and never mentioned my name."

"Your idea?" She tucked her phone in the pocket of her blazer.

Don't play dumb, bitch.

"Yes, I brought it up in our last meeting with Maurice and his team."

"Oh, Winnie at Code it's really about collaboration. We were brainstorming. You had ideas, I had ideas."

I narrowed my eyes. "That wasn't a brainstorming session and even if it was, that would make Meals with Miles *our* idea not solely yours."

"It's not about taking credit, it's about executing a vision."

"Perhaps, but it seems like your visions are always created by someone else. And because you didn't give me proper credit, now Miles thinks the idea was yours alone. When it wasn't your idea at all. That's just ... dishonest."

"I've been with this company for two years. I don't need to steal ideas from someone who gawks like a dullard when the robotic butler rolls past."

In my defense, it was a robot no bigger than a trash can rolling around the office. I was just waiting for it to walk into a wall or start the robot uprising.

"I can assure you being an executive assistant for two years isn't the flex you think it is."

"Honestly Winnie, a closed mouth doesn't get fed and you spend far too much time biting your tongue. Some people are doers while others will spend their whole lives watching from the sidelines."

"I've spent the last four months trying not to step on your very sensitive toes. But now I'm wearing steel-toed boots, so you better watch where you walk."

"Are you threatening me?"

"No. But I am setting some very real boundaries. First of which you can fetch your own coffee. I'm not your fucking errand girl and that task is not among my job responsibilities."

"It's all a part of paying your dues. It's not my problem you can't keep up."

I inched closer. "I can keep up. And you'll end up choking on my dust."

I swept out of the office, not allowing Jerrika the chance at a last word. Plus, I was running out of witty comeback lines. At my desk, I shut down my computer, grabbed my purse and went in search of Jamaal. After a series of text messages, I found him at the Lowe building. He came outside to greet me and I followed him to one of the quiet rooms. I was pumped with adrenaline rushing through my veins.

Finding it hard to stand still, I paced the length of the small space, recounting the conversation with Jamaal. "And then I told her ... listen here bitch I'm setting some gotdamn boundaries. I mean ... I didn't curse but you get my drift."

"That's good. That's all good."

"You should have seen her face. Shocked. Clutching pearls. Why is amicable Winnie talking to me like this? I'm not your errand girl, heifer. I said that I told her that."

"I'm assuming minus the word heifer."

"Yeah, no I didn't say that part." I shouted loudly, "There's a new bitch in town."

"Shh, quiet room," Jamaal reminded me.

"Oh yeah sorry." Dropping my tone to a whisper, I repeated myself. "There's a new bitch in town and she goes by the name Winifred Chambers."

I felt like I could run a marathon, or slap box a kangaroo. I needed to burn off some of this energy. Eyeing Jamaal, I locked the door to the tiny room.

"What are you doing?" he asked.

"I need you right now."

"Damn this new Winnie Chambers is a freak."

"The old Winnie Chambers was a freak too. Don't play with me."

"True. You did perform the most sensual hand job last night during Jeopardy."

"Well consider this your daily double." I was wearing a pleated skirt so I stepped out of my panties and draped myself over the two-seater desk waiting to get railed.

He wasted no time undoing his pants and letting them fall to his ankles before sliding inside. Grabbing hold of my ponytail, he used it as a rein to pump harder into my gushy center. The Lowe building was similar to a library or museum in that the structure felt cavernous and when a person spoke with any volume, their voice tended to echo. Even while attempting to muffle my moans, they seemed to ping off the walls and bounce back.

Jamaal leaned in, "Can you please be quiet."

"It's kinda hard to take the dick and be quiet at the same time. Which do you want?"

"If you don't shut up I'll have to put something in your mouth."

"I would actually love that."

Jamaal wrapped his hand around my neck and lifted me toward him slipping his tongue in my mouth. I moaned, greedy for more. He flipped me around and lifted me off the desk so he could continue to kiss me while we fucked. It was probably mostly to minimize my screams but I appreciated it anyway. I giggled with glee as he helped me maneuver over his length. The man who did not want to fuck me on the trampoline had no problems destroying my pussy in this eight by ten cube.

"Tell me you're a bad bitch," he ordered.

My body lit up at his words. "I'm a bad bitch."

"And in a year's time you'll be running this place."

I laughed at the absurdity of his last statement.

"Say it," he commanded with a thrust that compelled me to comply.

"I'll be running this place in a year."

"Whose dick is this?"

"Mine," I proudly proclaimed.

Jamaal dropped to a nearby chair and made me prove it and I rode his dick to a rolling orgasm with screams so loud they reverberated off the walls.

It had been a month. One glorious month with the man of my dreams, my fantasies, and my every waking thought. I could not get enough of him. We were on a double date with Risha and her husband, Harold. Whom I adored. They were funny and smart. Risha and I could talk for hours about food, crafts, and that reality show *Why Knot*, where participants marry a complete stranger. That left Jamaal to nerd it out with Harold discussing home-brewing or board games.

This is how I pictured a relationship, a melding of lives. Simone and Jamaal had also become fast friends, oftentimes teaming up on me. Which I actually hated. After much pressure from the two, I'd agreed to sign up for another run. They pitched it as more of a fun obstacle course with foaming bubbles. But perusing the website, it was heavy on the running and lite on the bubbles, which only appeared close to the finish line.

"I would like to make a toast," Jamaal said, lifting his glass of beer. "To Winnie who interviewed for the vacant social media position at Code and killed it."

"Here, here," Harold cheered.

"You don't know that I killed it."

"Of course you did." He turned to Risha and Harold. "She spent days boning up."

I giggled.

"You said bone," Risha teased. Our table erupted into laughter.

After confronting Jerrika, I realized I wasn't interested in fighting for scraps when ultimately, I wanted so much more. The next week I started monitoring job postings. Codeability usually posted internally before posting wide. Most of the positions were in accounting or HR but then a gem popped up. A job as a social media coordinator responsible for content posted on all Code sites. To apply, I just needed to have been with the company for a minimum of ninety days, which I had.

It would be a promotion, a boost in pay, and I'd get to do what I loved. More importantly, if I got the gig Jerrika would no longer be my boss. As you can imagine, since our heart to heart she'd been a royal pain in my ass. But I gave back the same energy I received, which I think unsettled her. One thing she'd stopped doing was talking to me any which way. So small victories.

"Why do you have that goofy smile on your face?" Jamaal asked Risha.

"I think I'm still shocked you were able to pull this delectable woman."

"What are you talking about? I have infinite game."

I laughed. "I don't know about that seeing how I had to kiss you first."

"All a part of his master plan, I'm sure," Harold said.

"Thank you. That. Exactly that," Jamaal agreed.

"Okay baby whatever you say."

Jamaal winked at me before giving my cheek a quick peck.

"So, I've been hearing that Code is looking to expand," Harold said. "Are you working on any of that, Jamaal?"

"No, I don't know much more about Code's future plans. Miles shared bits and pieces but it's hard to fit it all together."

"The mind of a genius." Harold took a sip of his mixed drink.

"Pfft," Risha rolled her eyes. "Geniuses don't steal ideas." Risha frowned. "I'm sorry he's not a genius but he is an asshole."

"He's not. He just ... operates from a different playbook," Jamaal said.

"And which one is that?" I asked.

"The playbook for backstabbers," Risha chimed in. "Miles couldn't run that place without you."

"But he is. He is literally running it without me."

"Jamaal, you created the essence of what makes Codeability so special," I reminded him.

"What's done is done. I don't want to be the guy who lets the past consume him. I got screwed. It was a hard lesson to learn, but I learned it."

"Miles may be the face of the company, but you are the backbone," I said.

"Noted." I'm going to go get some air." Jamaal kissed my forehead before leaving the table.

"Foot in mouth, Risha. Foot in mouth." Harold stood, following Jamaal outside.

"Your boyfriend is stubborn."

"I think it's less about being stubborn and more about being hurt. He trusted Miles with something really important to him."

"If it was me, Miles and I would've come to blows."

"It's different when it's family. And initially they didn't talk for months."

Jamaal had given me the complete backstory about Code and

how it ended up being launched by Miles. What started out as him sharing his idea with his cousin turned into late night conversations in which Miles would pick his brain on how it would work and the sustainability of it all. And Jamaal was so excited to have someone who seemed genuinely invested in his vision. Before he knew what was happening, Miles had filed patents and secured investors.

"Codeability is a billion-dollar company. I'd have never talked to him again."

"Look, try not to beat him up about this, he's already done that enough."

"I'm not trying to make him feel worse than he already does. But Jamaal is such a genuinely nice guy. When he joined Code, I found an ally. It can be difficult working in a male-dominated field. And while I'm more than capable at holding my own, it's nice to have friends who have your back. Jamaal could have chosen to align himself with the popular group, but instead he had lunch with me. And for the first time I didn't feel like an outsider. I just want all good things for him."

Jamaal and Harold returned, taking their seats.

"Jamaal, I'm sorry. I'm an idiot," Risha said.

"It's fine. You are an idiot but it's fine. I've grown used to it."

She threw her drink napkin at him with a chuckle.

"Who's up for a round of pool?" Harold asked.

"Oh, I am." Jamaal leaned in and asked me, "Do you know how to play pool?"

"No."

"Great." He turned to Risha and Harold. "Boys versus girls."

14

WE PARKED SEVERAL BLOCKS AWAY FROM MY PARENTS' house. It appeared my mother's summer soiree was well attended. I'd invited Winnie because we were at the point in our relationship where I wanted her to meet my family. We were practically spending every spare minute together, plus it was a chance for Winnie to get dressed up. And dress up she did.

Winnie was wearing a coral-colored dress that kissed her curves. Her long braids were twisted into two larger braids that wrapped around her head, forming a crown showcasing her delicate neck. On her feet were strappy heels that made her lean legs appear toned and elongated. As we walked up the drive, Winnie's eyes telegraphed her surprise. She tugged on my arm, stopping us in our tracks.

"Exactly how rich are your parents?"

"I believe the commoners call it filthy rich," I teased.

"I've only seen homes this large on TV."

"I know it seems overwhelming, but my family is just like yours." I gave her hand a soft squeeze in hopes of reassuring her.

"My family lives in an RV."

"And I'm sure it's very nice."

"It *is* really nice. Top of the line."

"My father is going to love you." I leaned in to kiss her shoulder.

"What about your mother?"

"Umm ... my father is going to love you." Winnie tugged free, trying to escape. "I'm kidding. My mother will adore you, because I adore you."

Inside, we dropped off Winnie's purse in the first-floor guest room before snagging two glasses of strawberry mimosas from one of the hired wait staff traversing the space with a tray. We then made our way to the expansive backyard which was decked out for the occasion. There was a step and repeat to my left, so the legacy families of Carmel Valley could feel like celebrities. Spread evenly across the yard were linen clad tables and chairs, and near the pool a bar was set up.

I located my mother in the center of a gaggle of women. When she spotted me and Winnie, she excused herself from the group. The smile that took over her face was radiant. I don't know if it was for me or Winnie, but I was always happy to be greeted by a smile.

"You made it," she said while enveloping me in a hug.

"I told you I'd be here." I turned to Winnie and introduced her. "Mom, this is my girlfriend, Winifred."

"Your girlfriend?" My mother's smile increased.

"Mother please don't."

My mother pushed me aside, clasping Winnie's hands between hers. "You don't know how many nights I've prayed Jamaal would meet someone. And here you are just as pretty as a picture," she gushed.

"Thank you. It's so nice to finally meet you, Mrs. Singleton. You have a lovely home. And you can call me Winnie or Winifred is fine too. Whichever you prefer."

"If I'm lucky maybe I'll get to call you my daughter-in-law."

"Whoa ... you just couldn't resist could you?" I said.

"It's fun watching you sweat," my mom teased. "Winnie, this party demands so much of my time. But we must get dinner on the calendar. I want to get to know all about you."

"That would be great."

"Okay you two go off and mingle and nosh. Jamaal, your cousin Miles is here ... somewhere." And just like that, she was off to spread her sunshine amongst her guests.

"Your mother is really nice." Winnie took a sip from her glass, a wave of relief washing over her face.

"I told you there was nothing to worry about."

"As always you were right. Mothers tend to like me. My ex-boyfriend's mother still sends me a Christmas card with a gift card each year."

"I think my sister is here too. You'll like her but you have to promise not to join forces with her and make fun of me."

Winnie cringed. "But there's so much material to work with."

"Like what?"

"Your ears."

"What's wrong with my ears?"

"Your ears are perfect." She rubbed her fingers over my ear, tugging my lobe. "They're just a little big. Dumbo like."

"Wow."

A strong hand rapped me on my back, interrupting my witty comeback about her wobbly knees. "You made it. Finally, someone cool to talk to." Miles crossed in front of me to give Winnie a hug. "Miss Chambers, you look as lovely as ever."

I rolled my eyes. He always felt the need to put on this fake charming persona. His entire life was just a series of make believe.

"Jamaal, do you think I could holler at you real quick?"

"I'm off the clock."

"Who said it was work related?"

"Then what's it about?"

"Okay you got me, it's work related. And it's private." Miles directed his attention to Winnie and shooed her away with her hand.

"I'll go wrangle us up some appetizers and maybe some more of these yummy mimosas," Winnie said.

I slid my arm around her waist. "You don't have to go."

"It's fine. I'll be back to rescue you in no time," she whispered.

I watched as Winnie made her way back into the house. That woman had no clue how devastatingly sexy she was. But I had plans on reminding her later. A naughty smile creased the corners of my mouth.

Miles snapped in my face and brought my attention back to him. "The expansion. I'm going to really need your help on this one buddy. I have the skeleton, but I need your input to add the ligaments, tissue, muscle, and flesh. We've always been a great team."

Miles was a trip. He'd already jumped out the window when he stole my idea and now he expected me to give over more of my intellectual property. "We've never been a team."

"What about that time we were in little league soccer?"

"Correction, we haven't been a team in years."

Helping Miles wasn't the priority and if I was being honest, some of the shit Risha said a week ago was still stuck in my craw. She was right, Miles took advantage of me and he would continue to do it because I was letting him. I was livid when he told me eleven years ago that he'd obtained a business license and planned to launch Codeability with the seed money from both his parents and mine. The asshole didn't even change the name. He just stole my shit part and parcel.

"You and I both know that you're my secret weapon," Miles said.

"Are you listening to yourself? Are you so oblivious that you don't see how fucked up it is to ask me this?"

"Fucked up? I'm asking for help. We're family and we should help each other."

"Help. Help. I think I've *helped* you more than enough."

Winnie approached with a plate loaded with finger foods. "I've brought the party back with me. Did you know they have the most delicious flatbread pizza with peaches on top?"

Both Miles and I ignored her arrival, continuing our exchange which left the blood coursing chaotically through my body.

"So all that best friends ... brothers talk means nothing?"

"To me it meant everything," I shouted, no longer able to hold it back. My elevated voice caught the attention of nearby guests. "I fucking trusted you Miles."

Winnie teetered between backing away and staying close.

"This again?"

"It's always going to be this. You never even said you were sorry."

"I'm sorry, damn. Are we going to be talking about this shit twenty years from now?"

"I don't know that this relationship will last through the week-end, let alone twenty years."

"Here we go. This is the part where Jamaal plays the victim. The truth is you were never going to move on Code. It was all talk, no action. You are and have always been a whiny punk ass bitch."

I cocked back my fist and punched Miles square in his jaw. My cousin stumbled back into a nearby table. I could hear Winnie scream next to me, but all I could do was lean into the rage. White, hot, searing rage.

Miles pulled off his linen jacket, tossing it to the ground. "Oh you want to fight. Well let's do this shit then."

"I want you to know this ass whooping I'm about to dole out is long overdue."

Miles swung and missed, and I tagged him with a punch to the ribs. My cousin was older and taller than me but I was scrappier. I also had years of festering anger to work through. Miles landed a punch to the side of my face before pushing me backward. Guests were scrambling trying to escape the melee in Carmel Valley. The sound of my father's booming voice grow closer, so I swung one last time connecting with Miles's jaw. Our fathers jumped in between us, pulling us apart.

"What the hell has gotten into you two," my father demanded.

"Oh nothing, just the usual. Miles Graves is a fucking thief."

"Your momma," Miles yelled like a twelve-year-old.

My father flashed him an icy stare which caused Miles's back to straighten. "Sorry Uncle Eddie."

My father dropped his voice so only Miles and I could hear. "Get your asses upstairs."

His tone transported me back to childhood and getting yelled at by my father after Miles and I broke something while horsing around. My dad did not play. Never had, never will. He was strict but fair. All it took was a single look, arched eyebrows, steely gaze with not a hint of humor under his bristled mustache, to convey his disappointment or anger.

As we headed upstairs, Winnie clutched my hand tight. She was still holding her plate of food. Now that my senses had returned, I realized that I'd ruined this afternoon for us. She was supposed to meet the family, not referee a street fight. We all filed into my mother's craft room. Miles, our parents, Winnie, and me.

"Boys what is this about?" Aunt Marsha asked.

Miles cleared his throat, the swelling from the punch to his jaw already showing signs of sticking around for a while. "It was a misunderstanding. We let it get too far."

"Jamaal?" My father looked to me for clarity.

"We just got our wires crossed." I bit down on the inside of my cheek.

"You two have never carried on like this before. And in front of my guest." My mother's voice was laced with displeasure. I could only imagine what her boujee ass neighbors were saying downstairs.

"Sorry Mom."

"Sorry Auntie," Miles echoed after me.

"You are both grown ass men. Talk it out and squash this shit. And don't come back downstairs until you do," my father ordered.

Our parents exited the room. Leaving Miles and I throwing pointy edged dagger glares at one another.

"I'm going to head downstairs so you two can talk." Winnie handed me my glasses, which were flung from my face during the fight. Offering an encouraging smile, she closed the door behind her.

"Was it worth it, hmm?" Miles asked. "Ruining your mother's party. Upsetting our family."

"Punching you in the face was worth it."

Miles breathed out a laugh.

"At this point I don't trust your ass as far as I can throw you. Family means something to me. And it just seems like you'd rather bulldoze over whoever to get to the top. Well, I hope the billion-dollar view is worth it."

"The view is shit. Don't be mad at me for sticking my neck out there and building the company from the ground up."

"If the vision for the company was your idea, the reward would be so much sweeter. But it's bitter ain't it?"

Miles shoulder twitched.

"You know why you suffer from imposter syndrome? It's because that's exactly what you are: a fake, a phony, and a con."

"Don't forget rich," he quipped. This was Miles's MO to deflect and pretend like it was all a joke for as long as it took until the other person gave up, gave in, or moved on.

"I'm done. Consider this my zero-day notice. I'm done with Codeability and I'm done with you."

"Jamaal, don't be ridiculous."

"I'm just taking your advice, cuz. You said I was a bitch baby who failed to launch. And you know what, maybe all of that shits true. But what I'm not is your fucking stepping stone." I brushed past him with a hard shove. Downstairs I found Winnie and said some curt goodbyes to the family who was still trying to salvage the party. We were halfway up the block before I slowed my stride.

"Jamaal, slow down. Babe." Winnie grabbed my arm. "Are you okay?"

I sliced my head from left to right. "No," I choked out, leaning into her hand that was now caressing my sore cheek.

"That was ..."

"A shit show. My mother is going to kill me for embarrassing her in front of all her friends."

"Maybe you can send her flowers to apologize."

"Flowers? Nothing short of a grandchild will appease her at this point."

"How'd things go with Miles?"

"I quit."

"Your job?"

"Yeah."

Winnie's eyes held a glimmer of tears. "I know I should be strong for you right now. But I think I'm going to cry because you're hurting, and I love you and I just want you to be okay."

Pulling her close, I let her sob into my chest. I was conflicted because the last thing I wanted was to burden Winnie with my dysfunctional family drama. But I also heard her say she loved me and that was paramount in my head. Not Miles, the fight, or what I would have to do to get back in my mother's good graces. I didn't even care that I was suddenly unemployed. If Winnie was in love with me, I could figure everything else out. When most of her wails turned into a whimper, I stepped back.

"Did you just say you loved me?"

"Jamaal Singleton, you are the sweetest, funniest, smartest man I've ever known. How could I not love you?"

"You make really good points." We both released strained laughs, still raw from the events of the day.

I scrubbed my face. "I don't know when exactly I fell in love with you. Maybe it happened all at once or slowly over time. But these past few weeks you have excavated my heart and taken up residence. You are all I think about. And I want to make you happy because you make me so happy. You're not alone, Winn. I am madly, truly, deeply in love with you."

She cupped my face, being mindful of my bruised lip, she kissed me. Even though it hurt I didn't pull back. I was kissing the woman I'd prayed for. Winnie reached for my hand and we continued our walk to the car.

"You beat Miles up," she reminded me.

"Yeah, he's a horrible fighter. He was always popular so he didn't have to learn how to defend himself."

"What are you going to do?" she whispered timidly.

"Well, I'm going to head home, take a shower, probably cry. And then I'll do what I've always done ... figure it out."

"We'll figure it out."

"I'm definitely going to need you to nurse me back to health. Miles hits like a five-year-old boy, but some of those blows landed."

"What did you have in mind?"

"Sponge baths and dick massages—"

Winnie pushed me playfully. "Shut up."

15

THE FIRST WEEK BACK TO WORK WITHOUT JAMAAL FELT surreal. I know we didn't work on the same floor, but the possibility of seeing him in the building or on campus throughout my day always got the butterflies to flutter in my tummy. On days when I wanted to burrow into the soft spot in my mattress, the thought of potentially running into him fueled me to get out of bed and start my day.

Jamaal was spending this week focusing on his Priority Desk pitch proposal. He'd run through his presentation a million times with me in the past few weeks. He knew the material front to back. So much so he could recite it in his sleep and on one occasion he had.

He understood the tech behind the software because he created it. And that man loved speaking his geek talk. I had no doubt he would crush the several pitches scheduled with financial backers who were always looking to get in on the ground floor of the next big thing. While I had no doubts, Jamaal wasn't so certain but I had faith enough for the both of us.

"Winifred, can I speak to you for a minute?" Miles called from the doorway of his office.

Jerrika's head snapped, looking up at Miles from her desk. I'm sure she was curious as to what Miles and I had to talk about. Not going to lie, I was interested too. I grabbed my notepad anticipating I may have to take notes. As I walked past Miles into his office, I noted the shiner he was sporting to his right eye, courtesy of Jamaal Singleton.

When the door shut behind us, I waited for a directive. Miles leaned on his desk and scrubbed his face. He didn't have his usually carefree and unbothered countenance. He reminded me of the man who showed up at Jamaal's apartment searching for reassurance.

"Maurice reached out to me the other day. He told me you'd recently interviewed for a position with Marketing and Communications."

"I did." I swallowed back the worry that was inching up my throat. *Uh-oh was I about to get fired?*

"He wanted to check with me before offering you the position. It would appear they are very eager to have you on their team."

My heart accelerated as I did my best to tamp down the smile curving my lips. I didn't want to get too excited if Miles was just going to shoot my dream down before it took flight.

Miles rubbed his palms together. "Does your wanting to leave have anything to do with Jamaal?"

I vehemently shook my head. "No this was something I've been thinking about for a while and I interviewed long before your disagreement with Jamaal."

He grimaced, reaching for the eye that was still visibly swollen from the blows Jamaal landed. "Why do you want to leave? Is it Jerrika?"

I was tempted to throw her under the bus, but decided against it. "I went to school for communication with a focus on web-based information. This is what I'm passionate about. And unfortunately the opportunities in my current role are limited."

"Well I'll hate to see you go. First Jamaal, now you."

"I'll still be with the company. And in all honesty, we never really talked until a few weeks ago."

"I was hoping we could all be friends."

"Maybe you should focus on rebuilding the relationship with your cousin."

I knew Jamaal felt a way about Miles even though he tried to pretend otherwise. But the last thing I expected was for them to come to blows. Violence was never the answer, but on occasion it helped to lead to a solution. Growing up, at times I had to knuckle up with my siblings to get my point across.

Miles released a long sigh. "I've tried and he punched me in my face."

"Have you though? Have you really tried to see things from his perspective?"

"I get that he's mad. But it's been years. I thought he was over that shit."

"Does one ever really get over being betrayed by someone they trusted?"

"Betrayed? I always intended for Codeability to be something for both of us. Jamaal and I working side by side."

"You pulled the rug from under his feet and then ran off into the night."

"With all due respect. You've only gotten his version of events. You haven't heard my side."

"I'm not the one who needs an explanation. And to make things very clear, as far as I'm concerned it's team Jamaal all the way."

Miles rose, crossing the room, he looked out his window. "Do you think he'd listen to me?"

"If you came to him from a real place of reconciliation and left the comedy act at home, I think he would."

Miles took a moment to consider my words. There was a world of hurt etched on his face, but I wasn't sure what all was behind it. Maybe it was regret for how he'd handled things. Or maybe deep down he didn't feel bad at all, but hated being seen as the bad guy.

"Well congrats on the job."

"Thank you," I said, heading for the door.

"Oh and Winnie?"

"Yes?"

"Do you think you could keep sending me those affirmations each week even though you'll no longer be my assistant? They've been really helpful."

"Yes, of course I can."

When I passed Jerrika's desk, she gave me the evil eye, but I didn't react. Back at my workstation, I grabbed my phone and went in search of a quiet place where I could share the good news with Jamaal and my parents.

That afternoon Maurice officially offered me the position, handing me a folder with an offer letter and more information about the Marketing and Communications division. I had three days to accept. Jamaal met me at my place and helped read through all the material.

"Just a word of advice. I would negotiate for more money. As Miles's assistant you have an insight into the mind of the CEO that few others have. You can leverage that into more money for yourself."

"Really?" The compensation seemed fair and I'd never been good at advocating for myself.

"Yep."

"How much more?"

Jamaal scribbled a number on my tentative offer letter.

"Seriously?"

"Yes. When you told me you applied, I researched the salary range for the market. You're worth it and they'll pay it."

I trusted Jamaal with my heart, so I knew he wouldn't lead me astray. Closing the folder, I felt uncomfortable talking about my new job when Jamaal's career was up in the air.

"Are you nervous about next week?" Jamaal had several meetings next week that could determine the future of the Priority Desk app. He was in need of investors which meant he would have to be persuasive, confident, and knowledgeable. Three attributes he possessed in abundance.

"I'm terrified. I can't remember the last time I didn't have a job. In junior high through college, I had my own tutoring service. I made up business cards and everything. I called it Best in Class Tutoring. That business paid for my food, drinks, and entertainment while at MIT with cash to spare."

"You're going to do great. You know that right?"

"I know that's what you keep saying." He rubbed my knee. "Winn, I just need this to work. I know I could apply at virtually any company and probably land the job but ..."

"You want something of your own. Something you created."

"I know it's crazy. But I've always wanted to run my own business and be my own boss. And create a work culture that allows employees to actually thrive, learn, and feel like a valuable part of the team no matter their role." Jamaal looked at me, his eyes swirling with uncertainty. "I don't know. Maybe Miles was right. Maybe I'm not cut out for this boss shit."

"No, what we're not going to do is entertain negative thoughts. I will not have you talking smack about the man I love."

"Are we talking about me?"

"Yes you. If anyone can make this happen, it's you. And it will happen. Maybe it's not next week, maybe it's a month from now. But I've never seen someone work so diligently to manifest their future. You are not just a dreamer, you are someone who gets shit done."

He brushed a braid from my face, kissing me in the way that made my toes curl and my body long for him. He pulled away sooner than I would have liked and I pouted to show my displeasure.

"Let's go celebrate your new job. I want to spend the rest of the evening gassing you up and fucking you senseless."

I blushed, wrapping him in my arms. "I love you, Jamaal."

He smiled. "It's crazy how I never get tired of hearing that combination of words. I love you too."

16

THE NEXT FEW WEEKS AFTER MY PITCH TO OVER TEN potential investors, it was crickets. I felt really good after each meeting. They asked questions, all of which I had well-crafted answers for. A few asked for additional information with projected output of the company in the first five years. Because I was an over-achiever, I provided them with a ten-year growth and revenue plan.

I believed in this company, and I just needed a few investors to bite. For any new venture to be successful, funds need to be acquired and I was willing to invest in the project, but that wouldn't be enough for Priority Desk to make it through the first year. There was Codeability stock I could cash out. That money would more than fund this endeavor, but having other individuals invest in this project would go a long way for the overall health of the company.

It was Wednesday, Winnie was at work and super busy because she'd started her new job. The steady downpour of rain had me feeling claustrophobic in my apartment. An apartment I was quickly outgrowing because Winnie was here practically every night. I'd packed up some of my things and moved it to a storage unit so she had space to spread out. Truthfully, I wanted her to move in right now, but she still had three months remaining on her lease with Simone and she didn't want to leave her high and dry.

If I had a job, I would've just paid the three months in advance.

But I was unemployed now. I wasn't struggling for money because I'd always been fiscally conservative, but I didn't think it was the right time to spend large sums of money when I didn't have a guaranteed way to make that money back.

I decided to check my emails for the fifth time that day. At the top of my inbox was an email from Kristoff Kringle. Kristoff was a tech guy who made millions off a word puzzle game he ended up selling to the *New York Times*. He'd made most of his money from creating apps. In his email he was offering to invest two hundred and fifty thousand dollars into Priority Desk.

I read the email through a dozen times looking for the catch. There was none. He was willing to invest the money and accept the terms I'd outlined in my pitch as to the return-on-investment timetable. My heart was pounding out of my chest and I needed to stand up and take several laps around the apartment to wrap my brain around everything.

I shot a quick text message to Winnie asking her to call me on her lunch break. To my great surprise, my phone rang almost immediately.

"Hey baby you didn't have to call me right now."

"It's cool. I'm on a break. What's up?"

"Are you sitting down?"

"No, I'm walking through campus. Why?"

"I just got an email from Kristoff Kringle."

"Kringle? Any relation to the North Pole Kringles?"

"Winn, I'm going to need you to focus."

"Sorry," she chuckled. Making me wish she was in the room with me so I could witness her nose wrinkle as she laughed.

"Anyway, Kristoff just agreed to invest two hundred and fifty thousand dollars into Priority Desk."

"Are you shitting me right now?"

"I'm not."

Winnie squealed so loudly I had to remove the phone from my ear. "Baby, I'm so proud of you," she cooed.

"Thank you. This is major. I mean I'm still going to need some of these other investors to chime in, but two hundred and fifty K is a hell of a start."

Winnie hyped me up for the remainder of the call, telling me how smart I was and calling me a visionary. She had a way of making me feel ten feet tall even when I'd been at my lowest these past few weeks. After my call with Winnie, I headed over to my parents' house.

My mother asked me to stop by at one o'clock. She needed help with some technical issues with the touchscreen intercoms. After showing my ass at her event I'd reached out to her and had to promise her five family dinners, a handful of date nights with my parents and Winnie and a two-hour IT class for her and her friends about how to get the most out of their smartphones and tablets. She forgave me with a warning that if I ever embarrassed her like that again, she would whoop my tail. I vowed to act right because that woman has a heavy hand.

"Mom," I called, using my key to let myself in. There was no response. Walking over to the intercom, I pressed the speaker button. "Will Phyllis Singleton report to the foyer. Mrs. Singleton your presence is needed in the foyer."

"Why are you playing on that thing?" My mother's voice called from the stairs.

"I thought you said it was broken?"

"Did I say that?"

"You said you were having issues."

"I did."

"So what's the issue?"

"Well dang, can't I get a hug and a kiss in first? You young people are always in such a rush. Where's the fire?"

"My bad." At the stairs landing, I wrapped my arms around her, kissing the top of her curly head.

Pulling away, she looked up at me. "Are we still on for our double date this Saturday?"

"Yes ma'am. We are looking forward to it."

"We," she chuckled. "You've been a *me* for so long now I have to get used to you being part of a *we*."

"You're not the only one."

"She's a nice girl. The type you marry and settle down with."

"She is all those things."

"We can have the engagement party here."

"Mom, why are the elders always in such a rush? Where is the fire?" I teased.

My mother kissed her teeth. "I want to play with my grand-kids. I want to go to ballet recitals, soccer games, and science fairs."

"How did we jump from engagement to babies?"

"It's not a jump, it's a natural progression. What does her family do?"

"They're circus people."

"Hmm ... well I like her all the same."

"So the intercom?"

"About that. Baby there's nothing wrong with the intercom. Your cousin Miles is in the backyard, and I would really appreciate it if you'd go out there and talk to him."

"Did he put you up to this?" I backed up, inching toward the door.

"He asked for my help, yes."

"I don't have anything more to say to him. Miles is right. I need to let Codeability go and move on with my life and that is exactly what I'm doing?"

"Without your cousin? Ever since you were born you two have been inseparable. I remember Miles meeting you for the first time when we brought you home. He could barely speak but he said 'My brother,' in the cutest little voice. He loved you from the moment he set eyes on you. He's family, he's my nephew, and I need you two to reconcile. And I don't mean fake amends to appease your mother. It doesn't sit right in my spirit knowing you two are at odds."

I rubbed my forehead sensing the beginning of a headache forming.

"I know he hurt you and it was a shitty thing to do."

I raised an eyebrow in surprise at her foul language.

"Yes, I said shitty. But just listen to what he has to say. Please."

I was never going to say no to my mother. I rolled my shoulders and cracked my knuckles. "Okay, I'll talk to him." I took slow steps toward the yard.

"And don't hit him," my mother called after me.

I found Miles under the covered patio. The rain had settled into a light sprinkle.

"Hey." He offered a nod to acknowledge my presence.

"Hey." I took a seat across from him. I didn't have shit to say so I decided to let him do the talking.

"How long are you going to be mad at me?"

All I had for him was an indifferent shrug.

"Okay." He pinned his arms against his chest. "Did I steal Codeability from you? Yes, I did. I never expected it to take off like it did. And for me to be named one of the richest people under forty or to end up on the cover of *Forbes* or *The Wall Street Journal*. I didn't think I'd be sleeping with supermodels, or hanging with Deion McCabe at the All-Star Game, or O'Keefe at the Superbowl. I never thought I'd have a private jet—"

"Is this supposed to be an apology? Cause it sounds like you're trying to pour salt on the wounds."

He planted his face into his hands with a sigh. "You have always been the smartest person in the room. I knew when you were five we were not the same. Everything came easier for you."

"Pfft."

"You never had to study. You barely even tried and you were top of your class. You got into MIT because you were fucking brilliant. I got into MIT because my parents are rich. And while attending that institution I could barely keep my head above water. I was cheating on my exams, having other people write my essays, I paid a dude to do all my homework. And what were you doing at MIT? You were running a tutoring business.

"Because of who my parents were I had the privilege of failing up. But I wanted to do something that would pull me out of Marsha and Trent's shadow and Codeability was just the thing. You were a junior in college and I thought I could do you a huge favor and get this company up and running for when you graduated."

"By launching my business in total secrecy?"

"It was supposed to be a surprise."

"Sounds more like a stealth takeover to me."

"When you found out you were so upset."

"You're acting like we're fussing over a sandwich or something. Miles you stole my intellectual property and used it for your own personal gain."

"It didn't start out like that."

"Why can't you just say you're sorry." I jumped from my chair. "Just fucking apologize. I am so sick and tired of your excuses."

"I want to apologize but I feel like you're still not going to forgive me. Then what? We just go our separate ways. Ignore one another at family gatherings? You just move on with your life and get married and have kids and I'm just not part of any of that?"

"Maybe it's just for the best."

"What's for the best ... us being strangers?"

"I love you Miles but I don't always like you. You are a user and you don't respect boundaries."

"Okay, is it my turn to talk?"

"Knock yourself out."

"You're my best friend. You may be my only friend. You're also risk adverse. You fuss over every detail, and you don't know when to pull the trigger. You and I balance each other out. Ying and Yang. You're cautious, I'm a rebel. When you cook you clean as you go. And I ...

"You leave the mess for someone else."

Miles leaned forward. "I am sorry about what happened with Codeability? And maybe you've just made your mind up and determined I'm a liar and that you can't believe anything I say. But I really am sorry for hurting you. And I'm willing to do anything to make it right."

Without hesitation I said, "Sign over half of Codeability to me."

Miles's visage cracked and his laugh was high pitched. "I misspoke. I'm willing to do almost anything."

I didn't expect Miles to sign away his rights to the company. And it wasn't something I wanted. I'd spend entirely too much time dwelling on the past. It was time that Codeability was firmly in my rearview.

Miles continued, "I would be willing to provide you with a onetime sum as compensation. I don't expect you to forget what I did. But I hope we can pivot ... and rebuild ... our relationship." Miles leaned back in his chair, eyeing me.

Despite myself, I released a chuckle. "I don't intend to be mad forever. I'm just hurt, and I've been hurt and resentful for a long while. And it's just going to take me some time to get over it. I appreciate the apology because I do feel like that was something that was missing. Look I'm not interested in going on a road trip with you anytime soon but I think we can eventually move past this."

It wouldn't be instantaneous, but I didn't want to completely eliminate Miles from my life. From now on, I would work on setting boundaries and communicating at the first sign of tension. There was a brotherly bond underneath the rubble of our relationship, and I was willing to rebuild if he was.

And in the spirit of reconciliation, something inside nudged me to extend an invitation. "If you want? If you're in town. I'm planning a little something for Winnie on the twenty-third of this month. You should come through."

"I'd like that."

"I'll text you the details."

I sat on the patio listening to the rain long after Miles left. We couldn't fix what happened overnight. It had taken us years to get to this place of frustration and anger. And I was partially to blame. I should've been more vocal about how I felt years ago. Instead, I did what I always did, pushed my feelings down and told myself I was overreacting and needed to let it go. Losing my cousin over this Codeability mess wasn't an option. Eventually we'd be in a better place, but it would take time and honesty to get there. I was hopeful our friendship would be stronger in the long run.

17

Jamaal had been secretive about our date tonight. His only directive was to dress up in formal attire. Simone went shopping with me and helped me pick out a beautiful floor length, one shoulder, purple dress that hugged my curves. I felt like I was going to an award show, and when Jamaal and I headed downstairs and a limo was waiting, I thought that might actually be our destination.

As we got on the freeway, Jamaal handed me a mini bottle of Moet.

"Limos and champagne?" I asked.

"Only the best for you?"

"I think the last time I was in a limo was at my Uncle Axle's funeral."

"I'm sorry to hear about that?"

"It was years ago. I was nine." I took a sip of my bubbly straight from the bottle. "Where are we going?"

"You'll just have to wait and see," Jamaal said, with a squeeze to my thigh.

"You look so handsome." I leaned into him, my hand resting on his chest. Jamaal was wearing a tuxedo. He probably already owned it because the tux was tailored perfectly to fit his lean muscular frame. Of course in my eyes Jamaal always looked sexy, but in this tux he was causing my temperature to rise. I was tempted to tell the driver to circle the block a few times so I could hike up my dress and ride his dick like a carnival attraction.

"I'm just trying to match your fly. That dress has your ass sitting. Do you hear me?" He licked his lips which was like an invitation to kiss him. I sucked his bottom lip into mine before sliding my tongue into his mouth. We groped at each other, moaning through kisses and shifting our weight trying to get closer while still in our seatbelts. Jamaal was the first to pull away but the lustful look in his eyes told me that was the last thing he wanted to do.

"Oh I forgot. I got you something," he said, as I wiped lipstick from his lips. Jamaal reached into the side compartment of the door and presented a plastic box with a corsage inside. The corsage was made of white and light purple orchids to complement my dress.

"Jamaal, they're beautiful." He helped secure it to my wrist and I spent the remainder of the ride admiring them.

When the limo stopped at a roundabout, I noticed we were in front of a high school. There was a swarm of activity with people dressed to the nines just like us entering the building. The driver opened our door and Jamaal helped me out of the vehicle.

"I'll text you when we're ready to leave," Jamaal addressed the driver before claiming my hand and walking me to the curb.

"What is this?"

Jamaal tossed his arms into the air. "This Winnie Chambers is prom night."

I giggled uncontrollably. "Prom night?"

"Remember when you said you never attended prom? Well, I thought this could be our do over."

"You planned a prom for me?"

"No. I was going to plan a prom, but then I got to thinking this had to be a thing somewhere. And sure enough, a quick internet search led me to a company that hosts adult prom nights.

So individuals can relive their heyday or like us, finally get to experience prom."

"And that's why you got me the corsage."

"It's kind of a big part of the prom experience. Plus, I'm hoping to get laid tonight."

"Oh, you're going to get laid, mister. I'm going to suck your dick so thoroughly that you will see the gates of heaven."

Jamaal inhaled a deep breath and once again got to licking at his lips. "I'm looking forward to it." He ran his hand down the side of my arm. I was going to have to invest in some adult diapers because this man kept me dripping wet. Just the sound of his calm deep voice and my pussy transformed to a 100 percent chance of precipitation for days.

"Are you ready to go in?"

"Yes."

Inside, the school gymnasium was decorated just like all the proms I'd watched on television. With streamers, balloons and hand painted images on large brown stock paper. There was also a fully stocked bar so we could get our drink on. The theme was Hollywood Glam and Jamaal and I fit right in.

"Jamaal," a familiar voice called from behind us. It was Risha with Harold walking hand in hand.

"Oh my God what are you guys doing here?" I exclaimed.

"Jamaal mentioned a prom with drinks and I said take my money," Risha joked. "You look stunning by the way."

"Thank you. You do too. I love that yellow color on you. And the earrings," I gushed.

"Is this where the cool kids are gathered?" Simone wrapped her arms around me from behind."

"Simone? What? Jamaal." I pinged from one face to the other trying to figure out how they'd been able to keep this from me.

"It's prom night. And close friends kind of goes with that theme," he offered.

Simone was not alone, standing behind her was a tall, fine, ginger-haired fella.

"You must be Josh," I beamed, excited to meet the guy I'd been receiving weekly updates on.

Josh shook my hand. "Yes, nice to meet you. Congratulations on graduating from high school."

Simone rolled her eyes in his direction, whispering so only I could hear. "He's fine but kind of slow."

"But he's really good looking."

"That's exactly why I haven't dumped him yet. But I fear we are not long for this world."

"So you knew all along about the prom? When you went shopping with me to buy a dress. When I was obsessing about what to do with my hair."

"Guilty," she said in a sing-song voice.

"I see you went back to the mall and got the dress you told me to put back." I eyed her suspiciously.

"Also guilty. But your purple dress was a showstopper. I wasn't going to let you pass on it."

While I was talking with Simone, Jamaal must have left for the bar because he came back with drinks and an additional guest. "Everyone, this is my cousin Miles and his date Alexis. Miles, that's Risha, she works at Code. She's one of the smartest engineers in the department. Her husband Harold. Over there is Simone, Winnie's roommate and her date Josh, and you already know Winnie."

Eyeing Jamaal, he was stone faced. I couldn't imagine Miles showing up was a coincidence, so Jamaal must have invited him.

Jamaal handed me a fruity sweet mixed drink, just how I liked it. After some chit chat which included Miles introducing us to his date, a drop dead gorgeous model from the UK, and Risha telling Miles how to improve the backdoor software that monitored something or other—*sorry I kind of tuned out the technical speak*— Jamaal put his arm around my waist and led me to the dance floor.

I swayed side to side to the up tempo Anjeni song that floated through the speakers. "So you invited Miles?"

"I did."

"Does this mean—"

"It means I'm trying."

"That's all anyone can ask."

We danced around singing the words to every song the DJ spun. Jamaal circled behind me and I whined my waist, poking my backside against him. The gyrating motion of my hips was met by his dick. It wasn't erect but it was erect-adjacent, and I loved the thought of his body coming alive for me. Jamaal always made me feel desired and like I was the sexiest woman in the room. And there was a world-famous super model here.

As the tempo of the music slowed, I turned to face Jamaal, wrapping my arms over his shoulders and caressing the back of his head.

"Thank you for doing this."

"You're welcome, baby. I know that the next few months are going to be hectic with me getting my company off the ground, so I just wanted to do something to show you how much I appreciate you and how important you are."

"So you're trying to bank away goodwill for the days you work late and ignore me?" I teased.

"Something like that." He flashed his brilliant smile.

"I won't let you ignore me. I'll just show up at your office."

"I would like that. We could have a quickie on the copy machine." Jamaal patted my ass.

"Sounds uncomfortable. That reminds me, I want to bake a batch of sweet treats for your team's first day."

Jamaal nodded, his expression turning serious. I was beginning to feel uncomfortable under his scrutiny.

"What?"

He reached for my face, caressing my cheek. "I love you, Winnie. The moment I saw you I thought 'Man if this woman just gives me a millisecond of her time I'll make sure she never regrets it.' And this ... us is so much more than I ever thought to ask for. Everything else in this world is just a bonus because I have you."

My eyes were welling with tears and I tried hard to swallow them back, but it was an impossible task. I'd never loved anything or anyone, outside of my family, as much as I loved Jamaal. And the fact that a higher power created him with purpose and intention and then aligned our paths to meet, just reinforced that I was one of God's favorites. How'd I get so lucky? Plus, he thought he was the lucky one for finding me which made it all the more perfect. My mother always told me to find a man who loved the sound of your restless sigh. Because if he could love you on Sunday afternoon while laying in stained sweats on the couch and watching a bad movie, he'd love you forever.

Jamaal wiped at my tears with his thumb. "Happiness hides in your smile. In the way you look at me. In our heated debates about the benefit of sleeping with the fan on or off. In the freckles that dot your nose. In the feel of your hand in mine. When I bring you coffee in the morning and you say a little something sweet from my sweetheart. It's silly but it puts a goofy smile on my face which I can't wipe off long after we're headed our separate ways.

"Happiness is the text messages laced with emojis and GIFs that perfectly encapsulate our conversations. It's the way you say my name after we kiss ... it's softer, richer, and filled with so much meaning. You are happiness. Being with you and the life we're creating is my happiness."

Just when I thought the tears were drying up, I found myself crying again. "All those things, I feel every single one of those things. I thought I was happy before, but with you I'm happy about today and excited about the future. I'm not as eloquent as you but I fucking love you and I have no plans of stopping."

There were no more words needed. Our lips connected as we swayed on the crowded dance floor. If this was a real high school prom a teacher would be pulling us off one another. But this was an adult function so I could fondle this man to my heart's content. My crush on the handsome man in glasses had led me to being loved and supported in ways I didn't know were possible. It was this moment and all the others that confirmed I would forever be in love with Jamaal, the IT guy.

EPILOGUE

THE PRIORITY DESK OFFICES CONSISTED OF ONE SUITE on the third floor of a modest commercial building in La Jolla. It was a departure from the expansive Codeability campus with perks and amenities. I kept reminding myself every company had humble beginnings. Apple didn't start as the dominant tech company; it took years of hard work. I'd never been afraid to roll my sleeves up and get dirty and right now that was a plus. With limited staff, I was tech support, accounting, copy editor, quality checker.

But Priority Desk was mine so if I had to copy, collate, and distribute infographics I was down. Winnie walked into the suite and it was immediately ten times brighter. I rushed to the front desk to meet her and empty her arms, which were balancing tins filled with treats. We walked over to the kitchenette and laid the items on the shallow counter.

"You do not have to keep doing this."

"I know but your staff deserves a sweet pick me up every now and then."

My staff consisted of a receptionist, five software engineers, one IT support guy, and Kathy who was a jack-of-all-trades in charge of customer support, social media, and human resources. We were a lean team and the six months we'd been in business, the focus was centered on preparing for the app launch. Once Kristoff jumped on board, several additional investors followed and I was able to secure funds beyond my initial goal.

After snagging a few treats, I walked with Winnie through the space while she greeted each employee individually and alerted them of the treat delivery which they all appreciated. Back in my office we sat on the thrifted couch.

"I still think you should have gotten something nicer." She sank into the well-worn cushions.

"We need to be fiscally responsible if we're going to buy a house."

Winnie's smile turned warm. "I liked the place we looked at last weekend."

"You like every place we look at."

She wrinkled her nose. "I know but what do you expect? Growing up my home was vans and RV's. So having a place you can't hitch to a truck is very appealing."

I popped a raspberry lemon cookie in my mouth. "I get it and we are going to find our perfect starter home."

She grabbed my cheeks. "Forever home."

"When Priority Desk takes off I'm going to get you a place in one of those gated communities."

"I don't need any of that. I just need you and our little love nest. Preferably with a backyard and a big tree."

I knew Winnie was special the moment I laid eyes on her, but I had no idea this woman would have my heart securely tucked in the palm of her hand like this. Everything I did was with her in mind. Starting this company, getting it to successfully launch. Finding the right home in a walkable neighborhood. I didn't need to be a millionaire, I just needed to be able to afford one of those retro stoves my baby had her eye on. *Trust me they were not cheap.*

Winnie pulled her legs up, crossing them.

"When do you have to be back to work?" I asked.

"I don't. I'm taking you to a late lunch."

"I don't know if I'm free." I glanced at my smartwatch.

"I coordinated with Kathy and asked her to block off your calendar weeks ago. You officially have the rest of the afternoon. Because you sir, are neglecting this thing called work life balance."

"Wow ... thank you for always taking care of me." I gave her lips a quick peck. "What do you have in mind?"

"Trust me I have tons of activities planned for you." She pressed her full lips to mine, using her tongue to emphasize exactly what was on the agenda. Winnie's phone made a unusual buzzing sound. "Oh that reminds me. When you have a chance can you look at my phone? The text messages are doing something funny."

"Sometimes I wonder if you're dating me for my dazzling good looks or my tech savvy."

"Why can't it be both? After all, it's nice having my very own in-house IT professional." She giggled, silencing any objection with a kiss.

Thank You. Let's Connect.

Thank you so much for reading Jamaal the IT Guy. If you enjoyed Winnie & Jamaal's story, please help a sister out and leave a review or tell a friend. Your feedback is important to me and will help other readers decide whether to read my book too.

Feel free to connect with me virtually. I would love to engage with you.

: @authorkashathompson

: @authorkashathompson

: @authorkthompson

HAPPY READING,

Kasha

About The Author

Kasha Thompson is a contemporary romance author. She writes authentic love stories that examine the complexity of falling and staying in love. Her books center black love with relatable characters, humor, and spice.

Also By Kasha Thompson

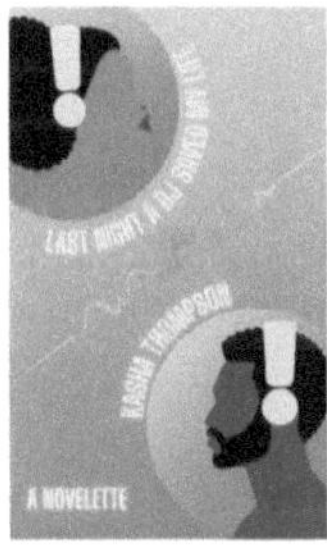